The woman came closer and poked his chest as she spoke. "You ran me off the road and totaled my car. I need to be someplace far away from here. All I'm asking is for a ride to the next town so I can grab a bus. It's all any decent person would do."

She sounded desperate, despite her strong stand. All his instincts told him to stay away. "Maybe I'm not decent."

"As long as you take me to the next town, your moral character doesn't mean a thing to me." She grabbed her suitcases and tossed them into the back of his Corvette. Something had slid off one as she hoisted them up. Quint bent to retrieve it. It was a wreath of white silk roses, partially crushed. It was the kind worn by brides.

D0172151

ABOUT THE AUTHOR

Mary Anne Wilson lives in Southern California with her husband, three children, two exceptional grandchildren and an odd assortment of dysfunctional pets. She has been a RITA Award finalist for outstanding romantic suspense, makes regular appearances on the Waldenbooks bestseller list and has been a Reviewer's Choice nominee for *Romantic Times* magazine. She believes real love is a rare and precious gift—the greatest mystery of life.

Books by Mary Anne Wilson

HARLEQUIN AMERICAN ROMANCE

MARY ANNE WILSON

THE BRIDE WORE BLUE JEANS

Harlequin Books

TORONTO • NEW YORK • LONDON
AMSTERDAM • PARIS • SYDNEY • HAMBURG
STOCKHOLM • ATHENS • TOKYO • MILAN
MADRID • WARSAW • BUDAPEST • AUCKLAND

To Mary Bignell, my mother and friend. Thanks for always being there through the good, the bad and the crazy. I love you.

ISBN 0-373-16570-6

THE BRIDE WORE BLUE JEANS

Prologue

Boston, Massachusetts

The item made the front page of the Boston daily in a three-inch double column near the top right corner under the banner:

Plea Bargain for Celebrity Bodyguard.

The former employee of local talk show host Gerald Darling pleaded guilty to felonious aggravated assault charges stemming from a brutal attack on the celebrity at his Boston home.

Quinton James Gallagher, 35, held without bail, faces up to five years in state prison after accepting the District Attorney's offer to drop the attempted murder charge and a possible twenty-year sentence to the lesser charge with a maximum sentence of five years.

On New Year's Eve, Gallagher rocked the entertainment world when he admitted attacking Darling and leaving him with broken ribs, a dislocated shoulder and numerous contusions and bruises. Gallagher alleged that he found Darling raping an unnamed woman. Darling denied all charges and the alleged victim failed to back up Gallagher's accusations.

Gallagher was hired by the talk show host three months prior to the incident and before that made a living at odd jobs that ran the gamut from handyman to security expert.

When informed of the plea agreement, Darling, now fully recovered from the attack, stated that he just wanted to put the matter behind him and get on with his life. "Justice has been served," said Darling.

QUINT GALLAGHER stared at the newspaper his attorney, Willis Gray, had folded and pressed against the Plexiglas partition in the visitor's room of the jail.

"I only agreed to the deal four hours ago and it's already in the papers," Gray said, his narrow face intense as he peered at Quint around the edge of the paper. His voice sounded tinny through the small microphone in the glass barrier.

Quint hunched toward the glass, his elbows on the narrow shelf and his hands clenched so tightly that they ached as he stared at the newspaper. His own reflection overlaid the black and white newsprint, an odd illusion. His short black hair was combed straight back from a face stamped with years of living on the edge. A ragged cut on his forehead had healed to a pink scar and his dark eyes flashed with cold rage.

"I should have let it go to trial," he muttered, anger clipping every word.

"And you would have been put away for twenty years. No one backed up your version, least of all the so-called victim." The attorney shrugged. "This way, with good behavior, you'll walk away in two years."

Quint sat back, letting his fists hit the table with a dull thud. "Walking out of here right now would be better."

"Considering the fact you almost killed one of this city's major celebrities with your bare hands, the only place most people want you to walk is around a prison yard for the rest of your life." Gray pulled the paper back and dropped it into his open briefcase before he snapped the lid shut, then grabbed the handle. He never looked away from Quint. "It wasn't a popular move for the D.A. to go to a plea bargain. You're lucky Darling didn't put up a fight to see the original indictment saved."

"Sure, damned lucky," Quint ground out.

Gray stood. "I'm going to talk to the D.A. about your transfer to the prison."

Quint stayed seated, prolonging the time before he had to go back to the suffocating cell. "Did you take care of the other things for me?"

"Everything is in order." He smoothed the front of his immaculate suit. "One last thing?"

"What?"

"The next time you get the urge to jump in and play knight in shining armor, don't."

"There won't be a next time." Quint stared intently at Gray as the attorney nodded, then headed for the heavy steel security door at the back of the room. "Every man for himself from now on." Quint watched the door shut behind Gray, then he muttered to himself, "A rule to live by."

Chapter One

May—two years later

Quint could feel his heart drumming against his ribs, but as he approached the release area of the prison, the only outward manifestation of his raw nerves was the way he gripped the plain brown bag that held all of his personal effects. He stopped at the head of a line of six men, six feet from the barrier, and looked at one of the three guards who stood between him and freedom.

"Gallagher, Quinton James." The man read from the clipboard in his hand, then looked at Quint to compare the picture on the prison records with the man about to be released.

The photo on the clipboard had been taken at the jail when Quint had been booked. He knew that the man facing the guard today was irrevocably changed from the man who had tried to kill Gerald Darling with his bare hands.

The man the guard studied was leaner, honed to sinewy muscle by a combination of the plain prison diet and hours of working out in the weight room. The scar had healed to a pale jagged line that cut down his left temple through his eyebrow coming precariously close to his eye.

His dark hair, streaked with gray, had grown long enough to lie on his shoulders and the beard he'd grown in prison had been shaved off two hours ago. He controlled his expression, giving away none of the heart pounding anticipation of freedom just feet from him.

He'd learned the hard way to keep to himself and stay out of other people's business, everyone in this world was on their own, including him. That harsh reality had been burned into his soul over the past two years.

"Are you being met or do you need a bus ride to the airport?" the guard asked.

"I've got a ride," Quint said.

The man nodded, then held out an envelope to him. "Release hardship money and your instructions for reporting to your parole officer."

Quint took the envelope in his free hand, then waited through the verification of the other men being released with him. Finally, the guard came back to the front of the line and signaled to the guard in the gun tower near the release area. The ten-foot high gate slid back with a low metal groan.

"Good luck," the guard murmured as Quint passed him and stepped through the gate.

In single file, the men walked down a narrow walkway, past a brick wall and into a broad parking area. Quint stopped as the other men hurried past him to greet their waiting loved ones—wives, lovers, children, friends.

No one was here for him. When he'd gone in, he felt relieved he'd left nobody waiting and worrying for him. But now . . . He averted his eyes as the gate shut behind him and squinted into the brightness of the early morning sun.

For the first time since he'd been brought here in chains and ankle shackles, he was locked out, not in. For the first time in over two years, he was in his own clothes, a black T-shirt, jeans and scuffed cowboy boots.

He raked his loose hair back from his face with his fingers and inhaled deeply, then he passed by the other released prisoners clustered with their families. He stepped out into the graveled parking lot framed by chain-link fence topped with razor wire and spotted the only thing waiting for him.

His car, a black Corvette convertible, looked the same as it had the last time he'd seen it. It hugged the ground, looking as if it were moving at top speed even when it was parked in a drab parking lot between an old sedan and a pickup truck. He went toward it, making himself walk and not run. But he didn't take his eyes off the car.

He'd notified Willis Gray about his release date and the last thing the attorney did for him was to order the car out of storage and have it brought out here for him. A man stood by the back fender dressed in a navy uniform with a patch on the breast pocket that read Parris Storage and Parking.

"I'm Quint Gallagher," he said to the man. "This is my car."

"Easy to say," the man muttered as he straightened up and eyed Quint. "I'll have to see ID. I can't just hand over a car like this without being sure it's the right person who's getting the keys."

"Got to make sure you aren't handing it over to some escaped serial killer, I suppose," Quint said as he opened the paper bag that held his personal property. He found his driver's license at the bottom of the bag and held it out to the man. "You can't be too careful, can you?"

"No sir, we can't be too careful." The man glanced past Quint at the gray and beige buildings behind the fence. He didn't bother to temper the distaste in his expression. "I've never delivered anything out to this place before."

"I wouldn't expect too many people have."

"You out here visiting someone?" the man asked as he turned back to Quint.

Quint looked right at him. "No, I just broke out and I wanted a fast car for the getaway."

The man's eyes widened. "What in the—?"

"Take it easy." He was actually thankful that he still had a trace of humor left in him. "It's a joke."

"Sure, of course." The man colored as he laughed nervously and held out the key to Quint. "Here you go. She's all yours, sir." When Quint took the key, the man pulled a yellow paper out of his pocket and read from it. "Says here there's two pieces of luggage and a cardboard box in the trunk." He looked at Quint. "You can check to make sure everything's there."

"No need," Quint murmured.

"Then here's the receipt. Drive carefully, sir," the man said as he offered the paper to Quint and turned to go. Quint opened the door of his car and slipped into the surprising freshness of leather and cleaner. The storage company had detailed it and it didn't hold any traces of sitting for two years.

He tossed his paper bag over the console onto the other seat, closed the door, then pushed the key in the ignition.

As the engine started up, Quint felt the low throbbing vibrate through the racing frame. Quickly he lowered the windows and the convertible top, relishing the feeling of the sun on his face. Open sky. Fresh air. His heart lurched in his chest when he realized that this was not a dream. He was alone, but he was free.

He drove toward the only opening in the barrier and slipped through onto the public road outside. He turned west, pressed the accelerator and felt the car surge forward. As he drove away from the prison, he relished the rushing air tangling his shoulder-length hair and stinging his eyes.

As he flipped on the radio to the pulsating sound of hard rock, he glanced at the envelope the guard had given him as he left. A few hundred dollars and parole papers. Since his only relative, his brother, lived in California, his attorney had made sure his parole had been transferred to that state.

He had seven days to report to the parole office in Santa Barbara. And he'd be there. This time he'd look out for himself, do it by the rules and get on with his life without taking on other people's problems.

"Every man for himself," he murmured when he spotted the sign for the route west. "A rule to live by."

Scarlet, Oklahoma—two days later

"I JUST HAVE TO SAY that this is all so romantic," Miss Thomas!" Marla Clark, the seamstress who'd driven out from the next town to the Raines estate, carefully knelt by Anne Marie Thomas on the Mexican tile floor of the guest house.

"Call me Annie," the auburn-haired woman in the antique gown murmured, tension from the past week of hurried wedding plans making her shoulders and neck ache.

The petite gray-haired seamstress stopped in mid-motion as she pinned the side hem of the ivory satin-and-lace dress. She looked up and met Annie's gaze in the mirror. "The mister says to call you Miss Thomas for now."

Annie closed her eyes for a fleeting moment, tempted to tell the woman that she hated being called Miss Thomas by an employee as much as she hated Trevor's parents insisting on calling her Anne Marie.

"Annie sounds so...so plain, my dear," Mrs. Raines had murmured with a faint wrinkling of her nose in distaste. "Anne Marie, now that has a nice sound to it."

Annie had kept quiet then and she knew that now wasn't the time to make any changes. "Whatever he says."

The woman looked vaguely relieved as she went back to carefully hemming the fragile gown. "As I was saying, it's just so romantic."

Annie closed her eyes tightly for a moment and took a deep breath, then opened them to face her own image in the mirror. Romantic? It should have been with the whirlwind courtship, the rushed visit to see Trevor's parents, the party to introduce her to important people in the county, and the giddy rush to get married.

But she felt far from romantic right now and, in a shocking moment of truth, she realized that her relationship with her fiancé hadn't ever been truly romantic. When Trevor had first walked into the restaurant in Taos where she was working as manager, she'd noticed him. With blond good looks, a compact build and a certain air of self-confidence, he'd stood out from the usual crowd in the upscale restaurant.

Only recently she'd realized that his self-confidence came from knowing he could do whatever he wanted to do. He was the only son of people who owned half of this county in Oklahoma.

She stared at herself, at her skin touched with paleness making a striking contrast to her deep auburn curls piled on top of her head and ringed by a halo of white roses. Her green eyes were filled with tension, and there was a vague unsteadiness in the set of her chin.

She was feeling prewedding jitters at their worst. Making a lifetime commitment wasn't something she'd agreed to casually, but it was for the best. When she opened her hands that had curled into fists and flexed her fingers, the heavy engagement ring slipped off and fell to the floor.

"Oh, ma'am!" Marla gasped as she twisted and picked up the two-carat diamond. "You can't lose this. It's absolutely gorgeous." She handed the ring up to Annie. "This just about tops everything, doesn't it?"

She held the ring in her hand and closed her finger around it without putting it on. The opulent ring went along with the Raines family reputation. Trevor Raines, Senior, and his wife Angelica were owners of a six-thousand-acre ranch and politically active in local politics. But all Annie saw was a real home for her daughter.

Since she'd had Sammi two years ago, her life had been guided by what was right for her child. And this situation wasn't any different. Sammi needed a father and grandparents. If Annie wasn't madly, deliriously in love with the child's father, that didn't matter. She and Trevor could get along, and maybe, someday, real love would come.

Maybe Sammi could wear this same dress on her wedding day years from now. It had been worn by Trevor's grandmother and his mother and was undeniably beautiful, fashioned from antique lace overlaying fine satin. Real diamonds trailed around the high choker neckline. The bodice was being altered to fit Annie's less than voluptuous measurements, and the waist was being tucked in almost an inch.

"We were talking about it just today, me and the cook, Mrs. Bryce," Marla babbled on as Annie stared at herself. "We all know about the Raines family and especially young Mr. Raines. Good-looking, wild, a real lady's man—"

The woman cut off her own words, then fumbled to regroup. "I'm real sorry. I didn't mean anything. You . . . you know, he's been one of the area's most eligible bachelors for so long, a real catch." She warmed up to the subject. "And you're the lucky lady who got him. It's all over about how he met you a couple of years back, then you broke up, then he went after you again and brought you back here, you and that little baby."

She smiled at Annie in the mirror. "Who would've guessed that Trevor Raines would settle down to be a husband and father? And that baby, she's just an angel. So cute, with blond hair like her father's and huge green eyes like yours, and such a pretty name, Samantha, just as pretty as the little sweetie herself.''

Sammi had been formalized to Samantha for the Raineses, the way they'd formalized her to Anne Marie. "Yes, she's terrific," Annie said and wished she was here right now instead of in Taos with Jeannie and Charlie.

"I haven't seen her around this week."

"My friend and her husband were here for the party and they offered to take her back to Taos with them until the wedding. They're like her aunt and uncle and she loves them. They'll bring her back when they come for the service."

"That gives you and Mr. Trevor time together. That's so romantic." Marla sighed.

That's what Annie had thought. Time to be with Trevor, but all it had done was make her lonely for her daughter and see how much distance there was between herself and the man she was going to marry tomorrow.

"It's all so perfect now that you're back together and getting married. What a lovely little family you'll be."

That was it. Sammi would have a real family. "Yes, lovely," Annie whispered.

"Is the baby going to be in the wedding party?" Marla asked.

"No, she's too young. She'd probably eat rose petals instead of sprinkling them on the carpet."

She smiled at Annie in the mirror. "And Mr. and Mrs. Raines would probably smile indulgently. They're really going to spoil that little girl. You know the old saying about money can't buy happiness, but I think it sure can help."

Annie hated the jarring thought of the money involved. It actually had little to do with her decision. The really important thing was the family. Giving Sammi what Annie hadn't had for most of her life.

Marla stood and put her hands on her hips as she eyed Annie from head to foot. "I think that's it. I'll just make a few changes, then it's all ready for tomorrow."

Annie touched the diamonds on the choker neckline. "It's a lovely dress."

"It is, but you make it look even better," Marla said. "Now, let me help you get out of it so I can finish the alterations."

After Marla undid the row of tiny, satin-covered buttons on the back, she eased the dress forward and slipped Annie's arms out of it. Carefully the woman held the dress while Annie stepped over it, then she put the gown on a padded hanger.

Annie reached for her robe and slipped it on over her panties and the special bra the seamstress had insisted she wear to give the gown a clean line. Marla called the strapless lace-and-satin undergarment a bustier. But Annie thought it should have been called a corset with its stiff stays and underwiring.

"Should I check in with Mrs. Raines before leaving to see if she has any last minute problems?" Marla asked as she smoothed a plastic shroud over the dress.

"She's not here. She went into town with her husband for dinner. They thought I needed a bit of time alone. Even Trevor's gone to see a friend."

Marla frowned. "He's not gone, ma'am."

"Pardon me?" Annie asked as she cinched the tie of the white terry cloth robe at her waist.

"Mr. Trevor, he's here. I saw him with that friend of his, Mr. Hogue over by the stables."

"How long ago?"

"When I went out to the car to get some extra pins." She picked up the dress and her tote bag, then looked at Annie. "If that's all, I'll see you tomorrow at two. That should give us plenty of time to make sure everything's right before the ceremony starts at six."

"Yes, it should," Annie said as she walked the woman to the door.

When Marla headed for her car parked by the house, Annie glanced over at the stables. In the late afternoon sun the sprawling adobe-walled building shimmered from the heat. She heard a horse whinny, then spotted someone walking at the far end near the main entrance to the building. Trevor was with his friend, heading for the arched doorway.

Annie waved as Marla drove off, tucked the ring in the pocket of her robe and went back inside just long enough to find a pair of sandals. A moment later she stepped back outside and headed across the grass toward the stables. She was glad Trevor was still here. Maybe if they talked, if she told him about what she wanted and what she needed, he could reassure her.

By the time she neared the arched entry to the stables, perspiration trickled down between her breasts and errant curls were sticking to her skin at her neck and temples. Quickly she ducked into the stables, into shadows and decidedly cooler air being stirred by huge ceiling fans. She almost called out to Trevor as she went farther into the dim coolness, but the sound of a raised voice stopped her after two steps.

"Come on, Chris, don't be such a jerk. I want to go into town and have a little fun," Trevor was saying. "You know—Janey what's her name. I heard she's back at the Alibi Saloon, and she's always been willing. Damn, she's hot. Always was. Always will be."

Annie could barely comprehend what Trevor was saying, and she moved forward, just far enough to look around the corner of the stall to see down the main aisle. Trevor was slumped down on a hay bale by some empty stalls in the middle. He was dressed in dark leather pants, a dress Western shirt of bright turquoise fringed in black, and he had a bottle of beer in one hand.

Chris Hogue was out of sight, but Annie could hear him talking. "God, Trevor, you're getting married tomorrow. What do you want with someone like Janey, especially now?"

"If I have to explain that to you, you are in trouble," Trevor said and sourness rose in Annie as he kept speaking. "I'm getting married, not dying." He swigged more beer before he muttered, "Besides, I didn't get a bachelor party, so think of this as my party, but it's a party for two."

"Party with Annie."

"All Annie thinks about is the kid." He shook his head, and his voice was beginning to slur. "Can you believe she won't sleep with me again until after we're married? She says it's going to make it more special. It's a little late for that, I'd say."

"So, you're going to blow everything for a roll in the hay with someone like Janey?"

"I'm not going to blow anything. I got insurance."

"What are you talking about?"

"I was out of it free and clear after Annie told me she was pregnant, at least until the old man found out about the kid. He found an old letter Annie wrote to me after the kid was born. She got my P.O. box from a card I accidentally left behind at the restaurant where she worked. I should have burned the letter, but I didn't. So it came back to bite me in the butt."

"What's this got to do with insurance?"

"The old man said I'd abandoned *his* grandchild. He blew up and told me to make it right or I was out of everything. He said he was fed up with me. That I was old enough to settle down and straighten up. So, what could I do?"

He tossed off the last of the beer, then lobbed the bottle over the wall of the nearest stall and Annie jumped when she heard the glass shatter on the cement floor. "So, I get married, look like a good son, and do whatever I damn well want to do when the dust settles."

"The insurance, Trevor, what is it?"

He shrugged sharply. "My folks mostly want the kid here. Oh, they like the idea of me being married and settling down, but as long as I give them their grandchild, they'll be happy enough. If Annie doesn't like what I do, I'll just tell good old Mom and Dad that I'm afraid she's a terrible mother for their grandchild and let them help me get custody. So, I can't lose."

Annie pressed a hand to her middle as she fought gut-wrenching sickness. This couldn't be happening. A fury she never knew she possessed came to life in her.

As she moved closer, she kicked a rake propped against the wall, and when it fell with a clatter to the cement, Trevor turned and saw her. For a second, he met her gaze and Annie felt as if she finally saw the real Trevor Raines.

His eyes looked cold and hard, then a calculated smile touched his mouth. "Hey, there," he said. "There's my bride-to-be."

She glared at him, vaguely aware of his friend saying goodbye and disappearing down the aisleway. All she could do was swallow hard to control her rage. Trevor had money and power behind him. And he wanted Sammi for his own ends. The idea of running was there, but something made her stand her ground as Trevor got to his feet and walked unsteadily over to her.

The smell of beer was strong and distasteful, and Annie hugged her arms around her middle. How could she have even thought they could make a life together? She'd been fooling herself in the most horrible way.

"Hello babe," he murmured and reached out to touch her cheek.

Before she could stop herself, she slapped at his hand to prevent contact.

Anger flared in his alcohol-blurred eyes, and color stained his skin. "What in the hell . . . ?"

"I heard what you said," she managed. "Everything."

"What are you—?"

"Go into town and find Janey what's her name. Have your fun."

He looked almost confused. "Janey?"

"I'm out of here. Do whatever you want to do," she muttered and turned to go, but he grabbed her by her upper arm and spun her back around to face him.

He might be drunk, but he was strong and his fingers bit into her arm. "You're not going anywhere. So, you heard what I was saying. Welcome to the real world. It doesn't change anything."

"It changes everything," she said.

He shrugged as his hold on her tightened even more. "What does it change?"

"I'm not marrying you. I don't want you anywhere around Sammi." His hold was painful and it made her clench her teeth. "Let me go."

He regarded her for a long moment, then he grabbed the tie of her robe with his free hand and jerked her hips against his. The moment of contact made the bile rise in her throat. "Don't you understand," he breathed close to her face. "I can do anything I want to do. And unless you go along with my plans, I promise I'll make your life a misery. I can even arrange it that Sammi is taken away from you—don't doubt it." He fumbled with the tie. "So, why not just sit back and enjoy things?"

He actually laughed as if pleased with the position he had her in, then moved closer and nuzzled her neck with his lips. She tried to twist away, but he let go of the robe tie and grabbed a handful of her hair. He jerked hard and snapped her head back until she had to look right into his face.

In that moment, Annie saw the real Trevor Raines. And it provoked a rage in her that was searing. "You son of a—"

He cut off her words with another yank on her hair, which brought stinging tears to her eyes. "Hey, watch your mouth," he hissed. "You'd better get a grip on reality. I don't have to marry you. I could take the kid and kick you out. You ought to be grateful I'm willing to let you stay around."

He was a monster. Growing horror at what she'd almost fallen into filled her, and she gasped, "Let me go, Trevor."

He glared at her, the blurry edge from the alcohol all but gone from his eyes. "Sure, and you can just keep walking. I'll take the kid and you'll never see her again."

In that moment her hatred of Trevor won out and she acted instinctively, balling her hands in fists and driving them as hard as she could into Trevor's middle. She felt the contact at the same time she heard Trevor's gasp. Then his hands let her go and as Annie stumbled back from him, she saw him fall backward.

His hands clawed at air, but he couldn't do anything to stop his fall. The next thing she knew the world shifted to slow motion. Trevor went back, his head struck the sharp metal corner of the stall behind him, and he slowly crumpled to the cement floor.

Chapter Two

Annie clamped her hand over her mouth as she stared down at him on the cold concrete. He wasn't moving.

She inched closer to Trevor, then crouched by him, but didn't touch him. Slowly, her hand lowered. "Trevor? Trevor?"

He didn't move, but she could see he was breathing and the fumes of stale beer seemed to be everywhere. Cautiously, she reached out and nudged at his shoulder with one finger. When he stirred, she jerked her hand back. He moaned, flung one hand out to the side, then he stilled again.

She stared at him, not sure if he'd been knocked unconscious or if he'd passed out or maybe a bit of both. Either way, she knew she didn't want to be around when he woke up. She stood and turned, half stumbling across the threshold, then out into the late afternoon sun and across to the guest house. She didn't stop running until she was in the coolness of the house with the door closed and locked behind her.

Then she leaned back against the barrier and hugged her arms tightly around herself, trying to breathe and trying to not remember her last glimpse of Trevor on the ground. His ugly words echoed in her, overlapping with the words he'd said when he'd shown up on her doorstep after being gone for two and a half years, in Taos two months ago.

"Marry me," he'd begged her as he held out the engagement ring. *"I missed you. I'm ready to be a husband and father. I want you and Samantha in my life. Come to Oklahoma. Meet my parents. And we can be a family, a real family. Samantha can have a mother and father and grandparents."*

She took the ring out of her pocket and stared at it on her palm. That's why she'd come here. Not for the ring, or for the money of the Raines family. She'd come because she'd believed that they could be a family. She'd given up any dream of passionate, undying love as a reason for marriage and settled for giving Sammi what she'd never had.

Now that was gone. She looked at the ring as if it were a poisonous snake, then threw it. Before it had stopped clattering on the hard, clay tile by the hearth, she was at the bed and reaching for the phone. Quickly, she dialed Jeannie's number and when the answering machine clicked on, she spoke in a rush after the tone.

"Jeannie, it's me. I need to talk to you and it's important. I'll call back, but—"

The line clicked, then she heard Jeannie say, "Hey, Annie, I'm here. I thought I heard your voice when we were coming in. What's up?"

Annie bit her lip to steady herself. "Jeannie, is Sammi there?"

"Sure. Hold on."

There was a clicking sound, then Annie heard, "Mommy, Mommy?"

"Hi, baby. Mommy's coming to get you."

"Mommy, come here?"

"Yes, I'm coming. You be a good girl for Aunt Jeannie and I'll be there soon."

She heard Jeannie saying, "Tell Mommy, I love you."

"Wuv you," Sammi repeated.

Tears stung her eyes, and she knew that she'd do anything for her child. "I love you, too, sweetheart," she whispered.

"Now, say bye-bye," Jeannie said in the background.

"Bye-bye, Mommy," Sammi echoed, then Jeannie was back on the line. "Hey, sweetie, tomorrow's the big day. We're going to fly out at nine and—"

Annie spoke in a rush, "The wedding's off." She knew what she was going to do. "Don't come here. I'm coming there."

"Annie, what's going on?"

"I don't have time to explain right now, but I really need your help."

In that moment she remembered just why Jeannie was her best friend and not just the owner and boss at the restaurant. Jeannie didn't ask any more questions or try to argue with her, she just said, "You can explain later. For now, just tell me what you need me to do."

"The most important thing is, please, no matter what you hear, if Trevor shows up there before I can get there, don't let him near Sammi."

"All right."

Annie closed her eyes tightly. "Just...just don't let him get to her, or don't let him take her. Call the police if he even tries to take her."

"I promise you, he won't get near her until you're here."

"Good, good," she said, her voice starting to shake. "Are you flying back?"

Flying would be the fastest, but she couldn't take the chance of Trevor looking for her at the airport. "No, I'll drive. I've got my car." If she was leaving she had to get out of here right now. There was no way she could face another confrontation with Trevor when he came to. "I have to go, but I'll call you as soon as I get clear of this place, and I'll tell you everything. Until then, just trust me and do what I ask."

"You know I will, sweetie."

Annie hung up and swiped at the tears dampening her lashes. She wasn't about to indulge in self-pity, not now. Quickly she packed, half expecting Trevor to come pounding on the door any minute. She grabbed a pair of jeans and a loose white shirt to wear and stripped off her robe. She stepped into her jeans, but when she tried to undo the bustier, she couldn't manipulate the back buttons by herself.

Short of ripping it off, she knew she wouldn't take the time to get it off. So she gave up, slipped the shirt on over it, did up a couple of buttons, then knotted the loose tail at the front. She put her sandals back on, then grabbed her purse off the bed, quickly stuffed her remaining things in her suitcase and headed for the door. She had three hundred dollars and a car, all she brought with her when she'd first come here with Sammi. That was all she was going to take with her.

Annie stepped out into the lingering heat and looked over at the stables, but there was no one in sight. She started for the multicar garage that sat between the main house and the guest house, half running over the grass. By the time she got to the side door and stepped into the dim interior of the garage, her clothes were sticking to her.

Passing the family cars, she went right to her old compact and threw her things in the back seat. She hurried to open the garage door, then got in her car and thankfully the motor started on the second try. Slowly, she backed out onto the gravel driveway, turned in the loop that went past the main house and stopped just long enough to glance over at the stables.

Trevor was nowhere in sight. She pressed the gas pedal and drove toward the open gates. As she drove out onto the highway in the direction of the state road, she checked behind her in the rearview mirror. He'd be coming after her. She knew that, but for now the road was clear.

As she met her own gaze in the mirror, she saw she was still wearing the wreath of roses in her hair. She tugged at the satin halo, freeing it from her curls and loosening her hair all in one motion.

As her hair tumbled around her shoulders, she tossed the roses over her shoulder onto the back seat, then carelessly brushed her curls back from her damp skin. It was then she realized she was crying despite her attempt not to. Tears had come silently without warning, the way her world had shattered today. She pressed the accelerator, willing herself to be as far away from Trevor and the Raines family as she could get.

She swiped at her face as she approached the intersection and slowed for the stop sign. She had never been one to dream very much, but she'd let herself dream this past month. Dreams for Sammi...even for herself. Now the dreams were over.

With a shaky oath, she pressed the accelerator and swung right onto the two-lane highway that led west to New Mexico. "So much for dreams."

OF ALL THE DREAMS Quint had allowed himself to dream while he was locked up, none approached the reality of driving through the dusky half light of Oklahoma in early evening, alone and free.

He took a deep breath, relishing the feeling of the warm air rushing past, and he didn't see the oxidized blue car pull out in front of him until he was almost on top of it.

He uttered a low curse as he acted on instinct, swinging the Corvette sharply to the left into the thankfully empty oncoming lane. The pungent odor of burning rubber filled the air with the high-pitched squeal of the oversize tires trying to keep a grip on the rough pavement. For a split second, Quint thought the car was going to skid sideways onto the far shoulder, but at the last moment, the traction held and the car swung back into the right lane.

The Corvette came to a shuddering stop with its front end nosing down toward the pavement from the hard braking, then it stilled, half on and half off the pavement. Quint exhaled in a rush, thankful to be in one piece, then he realized the blare of a horn was shattering the silence.

He twisted in his seat so he could look behind him, and all he could see was a cloud of red dust filling the air. Then the dust began to settle, and he saw the red glow of taillights from the other car. The car had nosedived into a side ditch and the back end was all that was visible from the road.

He hesitated, a part of him willing to press the gas and to get the hell out of there, but he couldn't quite do it. He pressed the gas, but not before he rammed the Corvette into reverse. The hot tires squealed in protest on the pavement as he backed up to stop within three feet of the old car.

Leaving the Corvette idling, he jumped out and went to the other car. From what he could see, the car was maybe a mid-seventies' compact with oxidized blue paint with primer on the back fender. It had New Mexico plates and it was hopelessly burrowed into the soft bank of a three-foot deep ditch at a thirty-degree angle.

Quint eased down into the side of the ditch, using the side of the car for support, raising more dust in the process. He grabbed for the driver's door handle to pull himself close enough to look through the closed window. Inside, the lone occupant, a woman with brilliant auburn hair, was slumped against the steering wheel. She wasn't moving at all.

He pulled on the door handle repeatedly, but all he accomplished was to send a shooting pain up his arm and into his shoulder. All the while, he never took his eyes off of the unconscious woman in the car.

Finally in frustration he hit the window with the heel of his hand. "Hey! Hey!" he shouted over the constant blaring of the horn. He struck the glass again and again, and just when he was about to go around to the passenger side to try the door there, he saw the woman stir.

Slowly, she eased back. The horn stopped immediately, then she raised a shaky hand to her forehead, tangling her slender fingers in the coppery curls. Quint struck the window again. "Hey, lady!" he called.

The woman turned, and Quint finally saw her face. Her features were vaguely blurred by the failing light, but she looked pale and delicate, with finely boned features, a dusting of freckles across a straight nose and full lips touched by pale pink color.

A deep red trickle of blood stained her temple and smeared onto her cheek where she'd touched herself; the source was a small gash near her hairline by her left temple. She stared at him with eyes that looked almost emerald in the dim light.

"Open the window," he shouted, making a circular cranking motion with his hand.

She closed her eyes for a fleeting moment, then as she opened them again, she looked down at her hand stained with her own blood on the tips of her fingers. Her skin paled even more, and Quint could see her hand start to tremble.

"The window," he yelled, banging on the glass again as he dropped to his haunches by the car. "Roll it down."

She flinched at the noise he made, then she turned and awkwardly reached toward the door with her blood-stained hand. Slowly, the window was lowered and she looked up at him, her eyes vague and barely focused.

Quint gripped the door frame and leaned forward, speaking quickly to keep her from going any further into shock than she was now. "Just take it easy. The door's stuck, but I'll get you out the other side."

She touched her tongue to her pale lips and asked in a husky whisper, "My car... is it ruined?"

She was definitely in shock to be worried about an old junk heap like this. "It's down for the count, at least until you can get a tow truck out here."

She grimaced and slowly sank back against the seat, muttering, "Damn, damn, damn. This can't be happening."

"I know the feeling," Quint muttered.

She turned her head to look at Quint. "Where am I?"

Oh, God, amnesia, too? Things were going from bad to worse here. "Oklahoma."

She frowned, finely arched eyebrows tugging together as her face actually started to regain some color. "I meant the road. What road?"

"The state highway. I don't know the number. You just pulled out in front of me and—"

"Damn," she muttered again, and moved abruptly with more speed than Quint would have guessed she could muster. She reached for the door inside, frowned as she jerked her hand up, and said, "It doesn't open from the outside," as the door swung outward.

Quint moved back to keep from being hit by the door and grabbed at the top of it to keep from stumbling backward into the dust. Before he could do anything else, the woman grasped the car frame with one hand and braced herself on the seat with the other. In the next instant, she'd levered herself out of the car and was steadying herself not more than two feet in front of him.

She was taller than he would have guessed at first glance, maybe five feet eight inches or so, with a slender figure shown to full advantage by worn jeans that hugged long legs and softly swelling hips. A white shirt had been partially buttoned, then knotted at her middle, but didn't quite hide the hint of something frilly under it.

Her lightly tanned skin was touched by a sheen of moisture from the unrelenting heat, and loose strands of coppery hair clung at her cheeks and throat. As he heard her take a deep, shaky breath, he looked up and he saw her high breasts test the soft fabric of her top.

With a suddenness that almost made him reel, Quint was totally aware of how close the woman was to him—and how incredibly potent that closeness was. She was nothing like the women he used to find attractive, dark, busty and petite. She was none of those things, but his body didn't seem to care.

God, two years in prison had extracted a high price from him, snatching away his freedom and a part of his life, but there had been another toll. Although there hadn't been any particular woman in Quint's life for a very long time...if ever, he faced something he'd pushed away for two years while he was lost in a world of coldness and pain. He missed touching softness and heat. He missed that unique sensation of being totally lost in another human being.

He'd heard about men getting out of prison and heading straight for a whorehouse, but he'd never thought about it. He'd never been a man to have a woman just to have one. Not any more than he'd ever been a man to find someone and settle in for the long haul. But right now he knew how much he'd missed and ached from the lack of a woman's touch.

This woman in front of him seemed the embodiment of everything he'd needed for what seemed an eternity. The sight of her and the closeness of her was bringing an unexpected response in him that was almost embarrassing.

He shook off the feeling and got back to the business at hand. "Stay here and I'll go see if I can find someone to help." He made his way up the side of the ditch and stepped out onto the shimmering asphalt.

Before he could do more than look up and down the deserted road, he heard the woman making her way up the bank behind him. When he turned, he almost bumped into her. In a flashing second, she was reaching out to him, and he had her by both hands to keep her from falling backward into the ditch.

As unpremeditated as the contact was, it seemed to culminate what had started when she'd first stood in front of him. In a single heartbeat he could feel every inch of skin touching skin, and it formed a heat that seared into him. The light scent of blossoms mixed with a hint of something he knew he'd dreamed about in prison. It was the sweetness that was unique to a woman, and its presence was almost unbearable.

Quickly, he spun to his right, and in the process pulled her up and clear of the ditch. Then she was standing not more than five inches from him, their hands still tangled and, in self-defense it seemed, he jerked back and broke the contact cleanly and quickly.

"I'll go and find a phone," he said, his voice sounding alien to his own ears.

He turned from the sight of her, but when he started for the Corvette, she was there, running around to stand in front of him and block his retreat. Short of colliding with her, he had to stop in his tracks.

"You're not leaving me here," she said in a breathless voice, her eyes darting past him to the road behind them. When she looked back at him, she said, "You can't leave me."

The softness of the coming summer evening cast shadows at her cheeks and throat and darkened the bloody smear at her cut. "I'm going for help," he said.

She shook her head sharply, making her rich curls dance around her pale face. "No," she said as she folded her arms under her breasts. "You don't understand. I can't stay here."

He tucked the tips of his fingers in the pockets of his jeans when the urge to touch her exploded in him. There was no way he was going to brush the curls back from her damp skin, or try to blot at the blood on her forehead. "Yes, you can. I told you, I'd get help."

She glanced back at his car idling a few feet from them. "You ran me off the road."

"After you pulled out in front of me."

"I'm not going to argue with you," she muttered and turned abruptly to head for the passenger side of the Corvette.

Quint went after her, catching up with her as she reached for the door handle. He stopped her by grabbing her upper arm and wished he hadn't. Damn it, he was one raw nerve and she was running over it in a horribly basic way. He drew back as she turned to look at him and he balled his hand into a fist.

"Okay, okay," she said. "I'll pay you. All right?"

"I'm not a taxi service."

She came closer and faced him toe-to-toe, her soft scent almost overwhelming. "Listen to me and try to concentrate on the facts. You ran me off the road and I need to be someplace away from here. All I'm asking is for you to take me to the next town so I can do what I need to do."

"Lady, back off," he muttered.

Anger flared in the green depths of her eyes. "Any *decent* person would do that much for me, since my car's stuck and probably wouldn't start even if I could get it out of the ditch." She held his gaze. "And you put it there."

It was gradually getting to him that this woman, despite her strong stand, was desperate in some way. God knew he was a sucker for a woman in trouble, he thought bitterly. The hairs at the back of his neck began to tingle in a way that he understood all too well. She *was* in some kind of trouble, he just knew it.

He'd been here before, helping someone he shouldn't have helped, and he wasn't going to be here again. He didn't want any part of it.

"Maybe I'm not decent," he murmured.

He saw a flash of something cross her face, maybe a touch of uncertainty, but it was gone as quickly as it had come. And she was back on track. "As long as you take me to the next town, your moral character doesn't mean a thing one way or the other."

Yes, she was desperate, desperate enough to plunge headlong into a situation that could have been dangerous for her. She was willing to get into his car without knowing anything about him. "It should matter."

She looked past him down the road, then when her gaze met his again, she changed tactics. She held up one hand in a gesture of surrender. "Okay, okay, you're right. I may be taking a chance, but I don't think you're some crazy who just made a grand escape from an asylum or from jail."

Her words were too close to the truth, and they made Quint uncomfortable. "Why not?"

"A person like that would have passed by laughing maniacally, or they would have stopped and shot me. You didn't do either."

"Don't tempt me," he muttered.

She only looked a bit flustered for a moment before she regrouped. "Okay, you stopped. You got me out of the car."

"I didn't really have a choice."

She regarded him for a long moment, then changed tactics once more. She shrugged sharply. "All right. Forget it. I don't have time for this. I'll walk."

He had to give her the fact that she didn't waste her time on a ploy that wasn't working. But this was ridiculous. "You can't do that."

"Why not?"

"It's too hot to walk, and God knows how far the next town is."

"Twenty miles."

"You're from around here?"

She evaded the question. "It's twenty miles."

"Then it's going to take you all night."

She folded her arms on her breasts again and he averted his eyes from the suggestion of cleavage it produced at the neckline of her shirt. "Then it's up to you. Give me a ride."

Every man for himself—and every woman for herself. He didn't need this. He didn't want this, but that didn't stop him from foolishly asking, "What's going on with you?"

She hesitated for a fraction of a second, then her lush dark lashes swept low, veiling her green gaze. Then she did it again. She changed directions in a flash, but this time she did it literally. She walked past Quint in the direction of her disabled car.

When she half slid, half walked down the side of the ditch to get to the vehicle, he was shocked. She was actually going to do what he'd suggested in the first place and wait here for him to get help. But that delusional thought lasted for as long as it took her to reach inside, then reappear with a beat-up old suitcase in one hand, a purse in the other.

He stood very still, watching her make her way back up the bank, using the side of her car for leverage. When she stepped out onto the road, she dropped the suitcase at her feet and something white fell from it into the dirt. He stood very still, wondering what he'd have to do to make her stay right here so he could send someone back to help her. That way he'd do the right thing, be on his way and never have to lay eyes on her.

Chapter Three

Quint watched her take a deep breath, then loop the strap of the purse over her shoulder and pick up her suitcase. She ignored whatever had fallen from the suitcase and headed back toward him, her eyes down. She reached him—then kept right on going.

She was leaving. Walking away down the road. He felt instant relief for a moment, then uneasiness as he watched her slowly making her way down the road, struggling slightly with her beat-up suitcase. Dammit, she was infuriating. "Hey, what do you think you're doing?" he yelled after her.

"Walking," she called without turning around.

"Come on, you can't do that," he shouted.

He saw her shrug, but she didn't stop. She kept going, her hair ruffled by the hot air, her slender legs covering the distance with a speed that surprised him. But when finally she stopped, brushed at her hair with her free hand, then regripped her suitcase and started off again, he'd had enough.

He looked around, then went back to retrieve what had fallen off her suitcase. When he bent to pick it up off the ground, he saw it was a wreath of white silk roses that were partially crushed and soiled by the dust. He looked away from the roses to the woman who was a good two hundred feet down the road now.

He jogged to the car, got in and pushed the crumpled roses into the side pocket on the door before he shifted into gear. He started down the road and, despite his better judgment telling him to drive right on past her and never look back, he found himself slowing as he pulled up beside her.

"This is stupid," he called to her.

She cast him a cutting glance, then lifted her chin a bit, never broke stride and didn't say a thing. He kept beside her, driving at a crawl with his right arm around the back of the passenger seat. He couldn't help but notice the way her top was beginning to cling to her damp shoulders.

"All right. All right," he said when he knew he didn't have a choice. "Get in."

She stopped immediately and turned. "How far will you take me?"

"To the next town. That's where you wanted to go, isn't it?"

"That'll do," she said as she approached the car.

Quint got out of the car and went around to pop the trunk, but before he could go to get her suitcase, she was right beside him, tossing her bag into the trunk on top of his things. Then she went around and opened the passenger door.

Before Quint snapped the trunk shut and got back in the car, she was settled on the gray leather seat with her purse on the floor between her feet. "Can we go now?" she asked when he looked at her curiously.

A trickle of blood was escaping from the cut again. He flipped open the compartment in the console, took out a wad of tissues and tossed them onto her lap, not about to take the chance of making contact with her again. "Here," he said. "You're still bleeding."

She balled up the white tissues, then pressed them to her cut. "Now, can we go?"

Beautiful and rude. What a combination, he thought, then muttered, "Why not," and put the car into high gear. It surged forward and they were on the road in seconds with the hot air rushing past them.

When his passenger kept silent, he chanced a look at her. She was clutching the bloodied tissue in one hand that rested on her thigh, and she'd turned in the seat so she could look past the high seat at the road behind them. Her hair tangled around her face, and as her eyes narrowed, she tried to catch at her errant curls with her free hand.

"Do you know what the next town's called?" he asked.

"Langston."

"What did you do, check a map?"

"Excuse me?" she asked without taking her eyes off the road behind them.

"A map, a piece of paper with lines all over it that are roads?"

She shrugged, a fluttery movement. "No, I just know it's there."

"You don't live around here, do you?"

"Why do you say that?"

"New Mexico plates."

"Oh, yeah, sure."

"There's nothing behind us," he finally said.

That brought a reaction. She looked at him, but didn't say anything as she turned in the seat and sank down to stare straight ahead of them.

"Were you expecting someone to be there?"

"No."

"Then what were you looking for?"

"Nothing."

Quint had been around enough people who were in tight situations in and out of prison to recognize someone who was running. "Whatever you say."

Annie closed her eyes for a moment, as if she could shut out his sarcasm by the simple action. Or maybe she could ease the pounding in her head and the nervousness in her stomach. When she opened her eyes again, she looked down at the bloodstained tissue wadded in her hand.

The image of Trevor lying motionless on the floor of the stables cut through her. Everything had gone wrong, but she couldn't turn back now. She had no options.

Her car was dead and she was traveling with a stranger whom she knew wished he had never seen her. She cast a furtive look at him. A psycho in a black Corvette? She knew that creeps came in all shapes and sizes and drove any type of a car—

Her hand tightened on the tissue. Then she brushed at her hair with her other hand as the strands stung across her cheek, whipped by the rushing air. Actually this man wasn't much like Trevor. Where Trevor had pretty boy good looks, this man probably wouldn't even be called attractive in a conventional way.

His features were sharp and had been etched with a rough hand. His jaw was strong, his cheekbones high and clearly defined, his forehead broad and his eyes shaded by short, thick lashes. He had a dark complexion, but he wasn't exactly tanned, which struck her as odd since he drove a convertible and it was summer. Maybe he'd just bought the car, or maybe he didn't have the top down much. Dark hair streaked with gray was pulled straight back from his face in a low ponytail. He looked...strong, volatile. And male—almost uncomfortably male.

Right then he glanced at her. The direct gaze from eyes that were the color of deep, rich chocolate, cut right through her. Unnerved, she looked away, but not before she saw the scar, a jagged line of paler skin cutting from his eyebrow up to his hairline. She struggled with her hair, brushing it back from her eyes and mouth. But all the while she could feel the man looking at her...hard.

"What is it?" Annie finally asked when she couldn't take him looking at her like that. But she didn't look at him. She kept her eyes on the range land rushing past the sleek car.

"Are you going to tell me what's going on with you?"

She finally managed to catch her hair behind her head with one hand and hold it back from her face. "You ran me off the road. What don't you understand about that?"

"You cut in front of me. Either you were in such a rush that you didn't take time to check the road, or you were trying to commit suicide. Either way, you've got big trouble, lady."

She caught herself before she turned and looked behind her again. "The only trouble I have is that you put my car in a ditch and that was my only means of transportation."

"What's your name?" he asked abruptly.

She thought about giving him a phony name, but before she could say anything, he spoke up as if he'd read her mind. "Make one up, if you want to. I just want to be able to call you something besides, hey, you, or lady."

"Annie." It couldn't hurt to tell him that much. When she chanced a look at him, she was thankful to find his gaze on the road ahead of them. "What are you called?"

"A lot of things, some good, most bad," he said, fingering the steering wheel with strong, square-tipped fingers. "But most people call me Quint when they want to get my attention."

"No last name?"

"Not if you don't have one."

Touché, she thought, and tried to come up with something to talk about except herself. "Nice car, Quint."

"Thanks, Annie."

She twisted in her seat and tried to cover taking a look at the road behind her by pretending she was giving the car the once-over. "This is the first convertible I've ridden in," she murmured as she saw a car pull out onto the road behind them. It was so far back she couldn't even make out the color, let alone if it was Trevor's Bronco.

She turned back to face the front as Quint snapped on the headlights to cut through the growing dusk. "Once you own a convertible, you wouldn't want anything else," he said.

"I bet it can really go fast," she said, the image of the car behind them etched with painful clarity in her mind.

"Fast enough."

"How fast?"

He glanced at her, his eyes shadowed by the failing light, and she was thankful she didn't have to endure the direct gaze. "Fast enough," he murmured.

She chanced a quick look back over her shoulder and felt overwhelming relief that the car behind them had turned off. The road was empty again. She could feel her whole body relax just a bit and, without thinking, she let go of her hair. The next instant her hair was tangling around her face, in her eyes and in her mouth.

As she fought to get it under control, she sank lower in the seat. "You wouldn't happen to have another hair band, would you?" she asked Quint.

He flipped open the middle console compartment and held out a band to her. "I don't suppose you're going to tell me what you're running from, are you?" he asked as she smoothed back her hair and wrapped the band around it twice to get it under control.

She moved closer to the door, fighting a sudden urge to tell him everything. For a split second she had the wildest idea that this man could be a match for the Raines family and a crazed Trevor, that he could hold his own with anything and anyone. But the reality was that she was a terrible judge of character. It was even possible that he knew the Raines family, or at least their name.

What would he do if he knew she was running from the heir to the family fortune, that she'd left Trevor unconscious on the stable floor? She couldn't take any chances, not when it meant the difference between getting to Sammi or being stopped and having to go up against the Raines money and power.

"I owe you for giving me a ride, but—"

He reached down beside him on the left and startled her when he pulled out the rose wreath she'd been wearing earlier. "What's this?"

She snatched the ruined halo of roses from him. "Where did you get this from?"

"It fell off your suitcase back there. I thought you might want it."

She looked at the soiled, crushed roses, a perfect reflection of how she felt about the whole wedding. "I don't," she said and lifted her hand, letting the wind snatch the roses away from her. She didn't look back as they flew off behind them.

"Not any more than you want to answer my question."

"My personal life doesn't come under the freedom of information act."

"Forget it," he said, making a sharp motion with his right hand. "It's none of my business."

She felt a strange sense of loss at his words, even though she was doing her best to get him to back off. She had to remind herself that it really was just her and Sammi. Period. "You're right, it's none of your business," she said and shifted lower in the seat.

As she settled, she realized that if she moved her head just a touch to the right, she could see the road behind in the rearview mirror. The Raineses shouldn't be back from their dinner for maybe another two hours, and Trevor... If she was lucky, he'd stay out long enough for her to put distance between herself and the Raines ranch.

Either way, she hoped she had a few hours. That was what she had to concentrate on now—making sure she wasn't being followed and putting as much distance between herself and the ranch as possible.

When Quint looked at Annie after she'd been quiet for what seemed a long time, he saw that with her hair pulled back, the sweep of her throat was exposed, as well as the ugly cut on her forehead. She was slouched low in the seat, obviously using the side mirror to keep the road behind them in view.

Annie was real trouble, and not just because she was attacking his pent-up hormones. He could feel her tension, and it only reinforced the fact that he didn't want to be any part of whatever was going on with her.

He didn't want to know about her problems. He didn't need to know. He just needed to get her out of this car as quickly as he could and let her take her trouble with her.

When he saw the lights of a town in the distance, he slowed the car. "Is that Langston?"

She sat up straighter in the seat. "I think so."

He almost asked where to drop her, then he found himself saying something that he hadn't planned on saying. "Why don't I drop you at a police station in town? We can report the accident and you can get some first aid for your head, then find someone to get your car towed."

The police were people he never wanted to see again, but before he could reconsider his offer, Annie sat up straight and said, "Don't bother. Just let me out here."

"You're kidding?" he said as he looked at her. Her paleness was even more pronounced now and her hand was gripping the door handle. "We're at least five miles from that town."

"I'm sure it's at least *three* miles," she said, her gaze meeting his without blinking. "But I want out right here."

He wasn't going to argue when he was getting what he wanted. So he slowed and pulled onto the shoulder. As he stopped, he shifted in the seat to face Annie, but he didn't have a chance to say anything else before she grabbed her purse and scrambled out. She turned and looked at him, her face touched by the gentleness of the night shadows.

"My suitcase?"

"Sure." He got out and went around to pop the trunk and get her bag. He carried it around to where she stood with her purse clutched in one hand and put the suitcase on the dirt at her feet. "Here you go, lady."

When she reached for her suitcase, Quint knew this was for the best. Hadn't he learned his lesson when he ended up in prison for getting involved in something he shouldn't have? Instead of telling her he had no intention of going to the police, he turned without a word and went around to get back in the car.

He was no knight in shining armor. Never had been. Never would be. But he was a man, and he wouldn't soon forget this woman called Annie.

But he *would* forget her. He pulled the car into gear, then drove out onto the road. He almost got away, a clean break. But something in him made him look in the rearview mirror, and he wished he hadn't.

Annie looked incredibly small and vulnerable in the early evening shadows with dust drifting in the air around her, the suitcase in her hand... alone.

"Every man for himself," he muttered. He pressed the gas pedal, making the car surge forward into the night.

ANNIE STOOD on the shoulder of the road as the Corvette took off raising a cloud of dust in its wake. She watched until the taillights faded into the evening shadows, then she took a deep breath and started in the same direction Quint had gone.

The police. The moment he'd mentioned them, her stomach had clenched and hadn't eased since. She knew the Raineses had more than money. They had power, and she had no doubt that their power extended to the police in the county doing favors for them. The party they'd given to introduce her to their friends and business associates had included the chief of police in Scarlet, the mayor, someone from the state troopers and a low-level federal government official. People with power and people who wouldn't hesitate doing a favor for the Raines family.

After what happened in the stables, she didn't doubt that Trevor would use whatever he had to use to get what he wanted. Maybe that would mean calling in the police. He could have already, and she shouldn't be walking on a main road exposed to anyone who passed by.

She had to get out of sight, and hitchhiking wasn't the ideal position to be in. She walked faster, brushing at loose tendrils of hair at her forehead that had escaped the band Quint had given her, and she accidentally touched the cut.

The contact made her flinch, but she could tell the blood had dried. Besides, a cut was the least of her problems. She stared into the empty night ahead, then glanced up at the dark sky where stars were just coming to life. And for a reason she couldn't fathom, she felt a sudden sense of regret that Quint had left her life as quickly as he'd come into it.

The man had forced her old car into the ditch and left her on foot without any regret. And he asked too many questions. Questions that were almost as unsettling as the man himself, who was big and dark as the night, with strong hands controlling the powerful car. And those eyes, looking at her as if he could see into her soul. That thought made her shiver, and she picked up her pace.

She didn't know what she was going to do now. With no car, she was a sitting duck. If she tried to catch a bus, Trevor could be having them checked, just the way he could check the airlines. If she cut onto side roads, she'd never get a ride.

The sound of an engine came through the night behind her, and she turned to find headlights coming in her direction. Before the lights caught her in their glow, she thought of diving in the ditch to hide, but stopped herself when she realized it was a truck coming. The lights were set way too high for a car, and the engine had the unmistakable knocking sound of a diesel.

As it got closer, she could make out a huge tractor trailer and impulsively she put out her hand and stuck up her thumb. Almost immediately she heard the hissing sound of air brakes being applied, and the truck slowed until it came to a stop just ahead of her.

She hurried up to the front of the truck, and right then the door swung back. She looked up into the dimly lighted cab and saw the driver leaning over the seat to look out, a bulky man wearing a baseball cap and smoking a glowing cigar.

"Need a lift, little lady?" he called out to her.

"My car broke down."

"Then climb on in."

She swung her suitcase up into the cab onto the floor, then reached for the side rail and pulled herself up into the cab that smelled of cheap cigars and stale coffee. "Thanks," she breathed, as she sat on the hard seat.

"Where're you going, honey?" the man asked.

"West."

"Then you picked the right truck," he said as he reached past her and grabbed the strap on the door to tug the barrier shut with a resounding slam.

Annie felt his weight across her thighs, and the odor of unwashed body and stale smoke assailed her nostrils. As he drew back, his arm brushed her breasts lightly and she recoiled, knowing she should get out and take her chances walking.

But before she could say anything, the man put the truck in gear and took off. Chances were that he was hauling into Texas or New Mexico. One way or the other, she'd get farther from Scarlet, and if she could get across the state border, all the better. She stayed close to the door, one hand just inches from the handle and her other hand gripping her purse. This wasn't a fancy Corvette or Quint driving, but it was a means to an end.

The man turned to her and exhaled a cloud of cigar smoke. "Name's Bugsy. What's yours?"

"Mary," she said, and pressed closer to the door.

QUINT HAD DRIVEN into Langston, a town that was little more than a widening in the road, and found a restaurant at the far end of the main street that was open all night. Behind a Western-style facade with a huge lighted sign for The Amigo Bar and Café resided a greasy spoon restaurant. With red Formica tables and vinyl-covered booths along the front wall, the restaurant side of the building held little charm.

A counter ran the length of the place in the back, and to its right, through an archway opening, was the bar, with tinny music, smoky air and the low din of conversations. But Quint was one of only two customers in the restaurant side.

He sat in one of the booths that lined the side wall, nursing his second cup of coffee and ignoring the remains of his cheeseburger. He stared at the knotty pine walls that were covered by a collection of old license plates.

When he spotted a beat-up New Mexico plate dated 1955, he thought of Annie for the hundredth time since he left her by the side of the road. He couldn't quite forget his last glimpse of her in his rearview mirror or why he'd had to fight the urge to go back and get her.

Damn it, she was running. And whatever it was she'd kept looking for over her shoulder, he knew she wasn't about to go to the police for help. He sipped the last of his coffee, then put the cup down on the table.

He hated the way a woman who was a total stranger kept nudging at his thoughts. And the way he could still feel the tightness grow in him when he thought of her standing in front of him on the road. Fool, he told himself. Stop it. Hormones were irrational. A woman was just a woman, and he couldn't do a thing for that woman. He'd found out the hard way that no one fought another's battles in this world and walked away unscathed.

Quint ran his finger back and forth over the healed scar on his forehead and exhaled harshly. He'd felt out of step since he'd left prison, as if the world had gone into fast forward and he'd stayed in slow motion. Being in the car had helped him adjust, buffering him from the rest of the people around him. Until Annie pulled in front of him.

As if his last thought of her worked a perverse sort of magic, he saw Annie walk into the restaurant. A large man in soiled denim overalls and a baseball cap strode into the room, the stub of a cigar in his mouth. And Annie was right beside him.

Chapter Four

At first Annie was partially hidden by the man's bulk, then she took a step ahead of him and Quint got a good look at her. The image he'd carried with him paled at the sight of the reality. Her high cheeks were flushed, her hair was loose again and tangled in rich curls around her face. Next to the giant she was with, she looked even more delicate and vulnerable.

The man followed her to the counter, then slipped onto the stool next to the one Annie took. Quint stayed where he was, just watching, wondering if this man could be the person she was running from.

The waitress came out of the back, said something to the two of them, then motioned toward the bar entrance and reached for the coffeepot. As she put two mugs on the counter and poured the steaming liquid, Annie stood, took her purse with her and headed toward the bar. The man with her watched her go until she was out of sight, then he reached into his pocket and took out a cigar. He wasn't going anywhere without Annie.

The man drank coffee and smoked the cigar while he constantly checked the entrance to the bar. Then two or three minutes later, Annie came back and took her place at the bar. She laid her purse on the counter, then gripped the mug with both hands and sipped some coffee.

When the man by her spoke, she shook her head and he moved closer, leaning toward her until he was inches from her face. His expression was intense through the haze of cigar smoke, and Annie eased back a bit and shook her head again. When she took another drink from the mug, the man slipped his arm around her shoulders and whispered something in her ear.

Annie twisted out of the man's hold, fumbled in her purse and took out some money which she tossed onto the counter. Then she stood, but the man, despite his size, was quick and he was on his feet, blocking her path to the door. He grabbed her by her upper arm and smiled suggestively at her.

Quint didn't have any idea what they were saying because the music from the bar was drowning them out. But he couldn't miss the way Annie was trying to pull free or the high color in her face. He'd thought she was in trouble in the car, but he knew she was here and now. And trouble was about six foot two and at least two hundred and fifty pounds.

Quint flinched when the man grabbed Annie by her other arm and jerked her to him, bringing her face to within inches of his. She squirmed, but the more she tried to get free, the more he seemed to contain her. And even as Quint told himself to stay where he was, to let her lead her own life and get out of her own trouble, he was rising to his feet.

He couldn't just sit here and let the brute intimidate her like this. As he started across the wooden floor toward the two of them, he tried to size up the situation. The man was a giant. But when Quint saw the way the guy's fingers were pressing into Annie's flesh, he knew he couldn't turn back.

He tugged the band out of his hair, pushed it into his pocket, then shook his head and took a deep breath.

"Hey, there," he said.

The man looked up, and when Quint met the dark fury in his face, he knew that he'd underestimated him.

Quint knew if he had the common sense of a jelly bean, he'd keep going and leave the building. But since Annie had barged into his world, he was painfully lacking in common sense. Right now, he was walking into trouble with a capital *T*.

"What's your problem?" the guy demanded around the cigar.

Quint stopped and looked him up and down. He knew that any man could be dropped with a heel to the kneecap, or a hard kick in the groin. And in prison when you faced off with someone, you hit hard, fast and dirty. But with Annie in the way, he couldn't do anything just yet.

"Yeah, there's a problem." He looked right at Annie. "I've been looking all over for you. Where've you been?"

She was staring at him wide-eyed, then he caught a flash of relief, followed by a glimmer of understanding. And she fell in with his hastily constructed plan.

"Oh, there you are, honey! God, it was awful," she gasped. "Some creep...he ran me off the road and the car...it's in a ditch. It's ruined."

While the big man was distracted, Annie pulled to one side and freed herself. The next thing Quint knew she came toward him and threw herself at him as she sobbed, "I'm so sorry, so sorry." Then her arms circled his waist and her body was against his.

His breath caught as she pressed her softness against him, and for a split second, he lost his focus. He forgot what this was all about, that it was make-believe and in a heartbeat, the whole world seemed centered on holding on to this woman in his arms.

"Please forgive me," she gasped in a tremulous voice, then lifted her face and the next thing he knew, she was kissing him.

What happened next was a devastating mixture of pure instinct and raw desire. When he felt her lips on his and tasted her sweetness on his tongue, he drew her even closer and kissed her as if it was what he'd wanted to do all along.

Every ounce of need that had been bottled up in prison was in the kiss, every unfulfilled dream and painful desire. For the first time in what seemed a lifetime, he felt alive. And whatever the circumstances, he wasn't going to argue about it. Not when he felt surrounded by heat and softness and shot through with searing fire. Not when she was responding to his touch as surely as he was to hers.

Then as suddenly as she kissed him, Annie jerked back and everything was gone. Her eyes were wide with fear, and he realized that the fear came from the other man pulling her back toward him. He swung her to his right as if she weighed no more than a rag doll, but kept a firm grip on her upper arm.

Before Quint could react, he saw Annie struggle to stand, then ball her free hand into a fist and swing it sideways into the man's solar plexus. The blow barely made the man gasp, but it gave Quint a momentary advantage.

He spun to his right and kicked his left foot straight at the man's kneecap. He felt a satisfying crunch under the heel of his boot and heard a raging curse as the huge man fell to the floor in pain.

Quint turned to grab Annie and get her out of there, but right then someone yelled, "What in the hell's going on?"

Three men came rushing out of the bar. A ruddy-faced cowboy looked down at the man on the floor who was holding his leg and moaning, then he looked at Quint. "What've you done to him?"

Quint held up both hands palms out, cursing himself for letting Annie draw him into this. "Hey, he started it. I was just helping the lady, and he—"

The man looked past Quint, then frowned. "What lady?"

Quint darted a look to his left, but Annie wasn't at the counter. He turned, taking in the restaurant in a sweeping look, but Annie wasn't anywhere in sight.

A sense of déjà vu hit him with the impact of a fist driven into his middle. What a fool he was! Annie had taken off and left him to deal with the mess. And heaven help him, but it hurt more than anything Gerald Darling or the prison system had ever done to him.

Quint looked back at the man on the ground, then at the others. He might have made another mistake, but this time he wasn't going to stay around and protest his innocence so some D.A. could lock him up and throw away the key.

"Look, I don't want any trouble."

"You probably broke this guy's leg," one of the bar patrons said.

As the others came closer to gather around the groaning man on the floor, their attention was diverted, and Quint took his chance. He eased backward toward the entrance, never taking his eyes off the cluster of people by the counter. He kept moving until he felt the door at his back and he slowly eased it back.

He almost had it open before one of the men looked up and yelled, "Hey, you, you ain't going nowhere until we get this settled."

"Yeah, call the cops," the injured man on the floor gasped. "I'm pressin' charges."

Quint didn't wait to hear any more. He turned and hit the door with his shoulder, hurling it open to crash back against the outer wall. He lunged out into the heat of the night, crossing the sagging wood in two long strides and bypassed the stone steps to jump over the low railing and down onto the parking lot.

His feet hit the heavy gravel with a jarring crunch, then he turned to his left and ran for the Corvette that was all but invisible in the deep shadows cast by the only tree in the whole area. He only had a fleeting moment to look around, but Annie wasn't anywhere in sight.

As he neared the car, he felt like a human magnet, drawing trouble to him on all sides. Just because he'd met a woman with green eyes and a stubbornness that seemed to throw her into harm's way, he was doing things that he'd promised himself he never would do again. Just two days out of prison and he'd broken every rule he thought he'd forged in stone behind the chain-link and razor wire fence.

But Annie was gone, and that was over. The kiss had been a diversion, nothing more, and right now he wished he had another diversion. But there wasn't any. He just had to get the hell out of here in one piece.

When he reached the Corvette, he would have vaulted over the door to get in, but as his hands touched the warm metal, he knew that nothing was over. Someone was sitting in the passenger seat, and he didn't need bright lights to know that Annie wasn't gone at all.

Quint stared at her sitting in the passenger seat clutching her purse on her lap. And a rage inside him erupted. "Get the hell out of my car," he rasped, his fingers clutching the metal frame so tightly they ached.

"Quint, I—"

"You're on your own, lady. Now get out of my car."

"You get in and let's get out of here. We can't—"

"There is no *we*. Get that clear, here and now."

If Annie had had any other choice, she wouldn't have been in this car again, but she'd been robbed of choices when she came out of the restaurant moments ago and found the parking lot all but empty. And not after that kiss; it had been meant to convince Bugsy but ended up rocking her world. And she couldn't allow anything like that to get in her way.

She hadn't known exactly what Quint would do when he found her here, but she hadn't expected him to be raging at her. Not when the taste of him was still on her lips, and she knew all she had to do was to touch her lips with her tongue to experience it again.

But right now the kiss might never have been. The man looked as if he wanted to lift her bodily and throw her out of the car. And she had no arguments left for him. *"There is no we,"* he'd said, and she knew the stark truth of that sentence.

That moment when she'd been shocked to see him coming to her rescue with Bugsy might never have been. And when they had kissed...well, that was gone now, too. *There is no we.*

"All right, all right," she said, bracing herself. "You made your point. I'll get out and leave you—"

Before she could get the words out, the front door of the restaurant crashed open and Quint twisted to look back over his shoulder as someone yelled out, "Hey, you, get back here! The cops are on their way."

Things were going from bad to worse. Quint turned and, with a muttered curse vaulted the closed door, slid in behind the wheel and pushed the keys into the ignition.

The engine roared to life. "Hold on," he told her and jammed the car into gear.

Tires spun on gravel, throwing it out behind them as Quint swung the car to the left. When he snapped on the headlights, Annie saw two men charging the car from the restaurant, waving their hands and yelling, but whatever they were saying was lost in the roar of the engine.

She felt the car fishtail on the gravel. Then the tires hit the pavement of the highway and squealed until the car finally surged forward into the night, heading west.

Annie gripped the sides of the leather seat as the speed built until she could hear a roaring going past her ears from the rush of air. Her hair was being teased wildly, stinging her eyes and whipping across her cheek, but she made no attempt to brush it from her face. She didn't let go of her grip on the seat until Quint eased off on the gas as the lights of Langston faded into the night behind them.

She glanced at Quint, his hair tangled and the deep glow of the dash lights casting odd shadows on his face. There was tension in his jaw and the way he gripped the steering wheel; despite the fact he was decelerating, she could tell he wasn't exactly relaxing.

He didn't want her with him, he'd made that clear enough, but she knew that her presence in his car wasn't the main reason he was darting looks behind them and taking quick, shallow breaths.

"What happened in there?" she asked.

Quint slowed the car even more as he rummaged around in the pocket on the console, then he said to her, "Take the wheel."

"What?"

He cast her a shadowed look. "Since you're in this car for now, help me and hold it steady for a minute."

She reached over to touch the wheel and was taken aback that the heat of his touch still lingered in the leather cover. But she gripped it and did her best to keep the car fairly straight on the road while Quint quickly raked his hair back to tie it in a low ponytail.

When he took the wheel again, Annie drew back and fumbled in her pant pocket to get her own band. As she managed to capture her hair, she said, "Well, are you going to tell me?"

"What?"

"What did you do back there to have them charging out after you and threatening to call the cops?"

"I hurt that guy's knee, and he wasn't exactly happy about it. I think that's enough."

"He deserved it," she muttered. "He's a jerk."

"I started to tell the men in the bar that very thing, but my prime witness to the incident had made herself scarce." He looked at her, the night hiding his expression. "Who was that guy back there?" he asked.

"A truck driver. He gave me a ride, then when I came back from making a phone call, he...he thought I should stay with him."

"What a stupid thing to do," Quint muttered.

"Excuse me?"

"Stupid. Hitching a ride with that gorilla was the most stupid, dangerous thing—"

"Okay, okay, you made your point. I shouldn't have taken his offer of a ride, but I wasn't in any position to be picky."

"Thanks for leaving me holding the bag."

"You had it under control," she said with a shrug. "I thought it would just get confusing if I stayed around."

"So you ran out and got in my car?"

"I left," she said. "Getting in your car wasn't in the plan, but after I grabbed my suitcase from his truck, I realized I didn't have any other options."

"Well, I do," he said. He slowed the car a bit as he glanced at her. "And you're right in the middle of every one of them."

She could feel her hands clenching into fists on her thighs, but she tried to keep her voice light. "If I'm involved, don't you think you should fill me in?"

"All right. You're in trouble, and unless you tell me right now what's going on, I'm dumping you on the side of the road, and I won't show up again later on to flatten a lecherous truck driver when he comes on to you."

"I didn't ask—"

"No, you didn't. And it won't happen again. But I think I deserve some sort of explanation for what's going on with you." He paused, then, "*Now* you've got options—tell me or get out."

Quint almost held his breath. He was certain she'd ask to be put on the side of the road, and it shocked him that that wasn't what he really wanted. Despite the fact he almost dumped her in the parking lot at the restaurant, the idea of seeing her in his rearview mirror again, looking like a waif by the side of the road, was immensely distasteful to him.

He could sense her moving, looking away from him, but she didn't tell him to take a flying leap or to stop and let her out. "You're right. You deserve an explanation, but I'm not in trouble. I've just got a small problem."

"Semantics," he muttered.

"Trouble is something you get yourself into, a problem is something you have to figure out. And I'm trying to figure out something."

"What?"

He heard her release a sigh, then she spoke quickly, "I was supposed to be in a wedding, and I decided not to be. It's that simple."

"Whose wedding?"

"A friend's."

"If it's that simple, what's the thing you have with the cops?"

"It's not the same thing you have about the cops, that's for sure."

That came from left field and shook Quint. "What are you talking about?"

"I saw the way the mention of the cops made you take off like a bat out of hell. You wanted to toss me right there, but you took off and that meant dragging me with you. I think you're the one who's got something going on.''

Quint tried to regroup. ''We weren't talking about me.''

''Maybe we should.''

''It's my car, my rules. We're talking about you. If you're going to be in this car, I have to know what you're into.''

''All I want is to go to New Mexico. That's it.''

''What about the wedding?''

''It's been called off.''

''So, you took off?''

She shifted in the seat and when he took a look at her, she was resting her head against the back of the seat, staring at the starry sky overhead. ''I had to.'' She brushed at her cheek and he could see weariness in the action.

Something in that simple action touched him, maybe in the same way a stray puppy's plight would have. That comparison almost made him laugh. What he felt when he was around this woman wasn't pity, especially after the unexpected kiss at the restaurant.

''Why did you take off?'' he asked.

''It was getting ugly, and I didn't want any part of it.''

He knew that feeling, but she was doing a better job of avoiding being involved than he'd ever been able to do. ''Just because you ran out on a friend's wedding, the cops are after you?''

''No, of course not. I never said they were after me.''

''All right. Where are you heading?''

''I told you before—west.''

''West as in New Mexico?''

"Yes, New Mexico."

"And what's there?"

"A friend," she said.

"Another friend?"

"Yes."

"Is that one getting married, too?"

"No, of course not." She shifted in the seat and said, "Can I ask you something?"

"I told you, I'm off-limits as a subject of this conversation as long as we're in this car."

"I just want to know why you stepped in with that truck driver."

He wished he knew the answer to that himself. "I've got a bad case of potentially terminal foolishness."

Her laughter came from nowhere, a soft, lilting sound in the warm evening air and a wonderful contrast to the feelings and events since he'd met her. He couldn't remember the last time he'd heard a woman's laughter, or how absolutely beautiful it sounded.

"We've all had that from time to time," she said softly. "Look at me, I got in the truck with that...that gorilla."

He looked at her, the sound of her laughter was nothing compared to her smile exposed by the soft lights of the dash. He'd all but forgotten about laughter and beauty in this world, but this woman was bringing them back full force. "You got out of it in one piece."

"Thanks to you," she said softly as her smile began to die. "You were great back there."

He looked away, hating the end of the gentle expression of pleasure. "Any man, no matter how big he is, will fall like a log if you get him in the knee."

"Well, I'd always heard it was another part of the male anatomy you were supposed to aim for."

He actually found himself smiling at that, an expression that felt as if it hadn't been used for a lifetime. "That works, too."

"I bet it does."

He regripped the steering wheel as he realized how foreign this was to him, a pleasant conversation with another human being. "Although let me give you a bit of advice. Hitting a mountain in the stomach isn't exactly effective."

"It was all I could think of doing at the time."

"It helped, actually. It took him off guard long enough for me to do some damage."

"I thought if I acted like I was looking for you and kissed you..." Her voice trailed off, but not before her words brought back that moment when her lips touched his. The car jerked forward as tension began to replace the ease of moments earlier. "I did what I thought I needed to do," she said in a rush.

"Forget it," he said, but knew that was easier said than done.

"I want you to know that if there'd been any other ride around there, I wouldn't have gotten in your car. And I'll get out as soon as we get to the next town."

"How far is the next town?"

"I don't know. But it can't be that far. If we just keep heading west, we'll hit a town sooner or later, and you can drop me at a bus station. Or if there's a car rental...anything will do."

"Sure." He chanced a look at her and she'd snuggled down near the door and her eyes were closed.

"What about your suitcase?"

"I put it in your trunk."

"Just make yourself at home," he murmured.

She sighed as she settled and Quint looked away into the night. A feeling suspiciously like protectiveness was sneaking up on him. It was something that had probably been growing since the moment he saw her slumped against the steering wheel of her car.

But even as his feelings for her began to change, he steeled himself to resist. He couldn't afford to get his emotions tangled up with this stranger... or with anyone. He'd take Annie down the road, get her on a bus or in a car, then he'd keep going to California and stay with his plans... alone.

When she sighed again as she settled into a light sleep, the sound ran riot over his nerves. Quickly, he reached for the radio, flipped it on and soft pop music swirled around him.

He drove for about ten miles with Annie sleeping by him as he tried to ignore her presence. Then he saw something ahead of them, and at first he couldn't see exactly what it was. But as he got closer, he could make out flashing lights clustered on the road in the night. An accident, he thought at first, but as he went even closer, he knew it wasn't any accident. It was a roadblock.

Chapter Five

Quint slowed the Corvette and swung off the road onto the shoulder, parking under the protection of some low-growing shrubs. He looked over at Annie who was still asleep, then glanced away at the flashing lights he could see through the leaves of the shrubs.

He sat there for a long while just watching and trying to figure out what to do. He figured that a brawl in a diner was hardly a reason for the police to set up roadblocks.

Then he looked back at Annie and remembered the expression on her face when the man at the restaurant had shouted that they were calling the cops. And the way she'd reacted when he'd threatened to take her to the police station at Langston.

He didn't buy her story at all. If someone was putting up roadblocks to find her, the implications were alarming. There was only one way to find out just how much trouble she was in.

He stopped himself from reaching out to touch her to waken her. The last thing he needed was the feeling of her warm skin under his hands right now, so he gripped the steering wheel and said, "Annie? Annie?"

As she was drawn from a light, dreamless sleep Annie realized the car had stopped moving. She rubbed at her eyes with her knuckles. "Are we there?"

"No, we aren't."

"Then what—"

She saw him point straight ahead. "Up there. Look."

She turned to glance in the direction he indicated and she didn't understand at first. Through the branches of the scrubby trees, she didn't see the glow of a town or lights from houses. She saw flashing lights in a cluster, their colors spotting the night.

"Wh-what's going on?" she asked.

"I think we've found the police or they've found us."

Her heart lurched. "What?"

"It's a roadblock." Then he shook her by asking, "Are they looking for you?"

"No, of course not. I'm not some criminal."

"Then let's drive through and see what happens."

But she didn't want to face the police. She didn't know how far Trevor would go. Until today, she never would've thought he'd threaten to take her child away from her. When Quint would have put the car in gear, she acted instinctively and grabbed at his arm. "No. Don't."

"Why not?"

He froze at the contact, and she could feel the tension in the muscles under his warm skin. What could she tell him? "I...I..."

"I'll make this simple for you. Do whatever you want to do, but we don't have much time in case someone saw me pull off the road. They'll send someone to check. It's your call."

She had an urge to tell him to turn around and hit the gas, but she couldn't. This was the end of the road with Quint and she knew it. The most overwhelming urge to hold on to him filled her, but she pulled back her hand and reached for her purse. "You're right, it's my call. I'll get out here."

When he didn't say a thing, she looked at him to find him studying her so intently she felt as if he were looking into her soul. "Are you ever going to tell me the truth?"

She could feel her nails biting into her palms as she quashed the urge to blurt out everything. But she couldn't. The stakes were too high, so she decided to tell him a slightly altered version of the truth. "It's nothing. My friend was getting married and found out the man was a real snake, so she called it off...and I had a fight with him. He blames me for it."

"Why, were you the one to talk her out of it?"

"No, she heard the groom-to-be talking to a friend and she found out some things that were pretty awful. So she called it off."

"So he turned the cops loose on you?"

"I'm sure this roadblock has nothing to do with me, but..." She touched her tongue to her lips. "I'm probably overreacting, but the groom knows people in high places and I just don't want any more trouble. His family could buy and sell the whole police department."

"He sounds like a catch," Quint muttered.

"He's a jerk." She reached for the door handle. "Thanks for everything, Quint. I'll leave you in peace as soon as you get my suitcase out of the trunk." She expected him to get out then, but he didn't move.

"Annie? Where are you going to go?"

She looked around. "I guess across that pasture area, try to get around the roadblock, then find a ride farther down the way." That was the best idea she could come up with right now. None of her plans were very thought out. Everything had gone awry since she ran from Trevor. "I'll play it by ear and try not to take a ride from someone like Bugsy the truck driver."

"How about someone like me?"

"Excuse me?"

"Go across the field, and I'll try to wait for you about half a mile farther down the road."

She felt as if she were hearing words she'd conjured up herself because some part of her wanted Quint to be there for her. But Quint *was* there, watching her, waiting for her answer. "Are you serious?"

"I said I'd take you to the next town."

"But you almost threw me out of your car back at the restaurant."

"I would have, too."

"But you didn't have the time."

"The fact is, I'm going west."

She wasn't going to question his offer any further. "Thanks," she said, so overwhelmed she could say nothing more.

"Thank me when we both get by the roadblock."

"I know I'm not supposed to ask any questions, but are *you* going to have problems getting past the police?"

"I hope not," he said. "But I'll find out soon enough."

Quint looked ahead at the cluster of lights. "I'll be waiting by the side of the road with the emergency lights on." He flashed her a dark look over his shoulder as he put the car in gear. "If you don't show up, all I can say is, it's been interesting, Annie."

"Yes, it has been," she whispered as he slowly eased the car back onto the road and turned on the headlights.

Annie waited until he was almost to the roadblock before she turned and walked into the field. Dry grass and weeds crunched under her shoes as she headed away from the road.

She walked quickly, thankful for the dottings of brush and scrub trees that she could use for cover. The warm air made her clothes stick to her skin. She never expected Quint to offer to wait for her, and it touched her. He had every reason to run and keep running as far as he could from her. But he was waiting ahead in the night, and she picked up her pace.

Quint slowed as he approached the police cars parked three abreast on the road. Cops always made him uneasy, but right now his heart was pounding and his mouth was dry. What was he doing when he'd offered to wait for Annie down the road? When was he going to get over the urge to protect others? He was becoming an expert at complicating his life.

As Quint slowed, he could see three uniformed state troopers by the grouping of white cars. As one of them started toward the Corvette, Quint saw Annie's purse lying on the floor and casually leaned over and pushed it under the seat.

Quint took a deep, steadying breath, kept his hands on the steering wheel and watched the trooper approach the driver's door, flashlight in hand.

He aimed the strong beam at Quint for a moment, then around the interior of the convertible. When he lowered the light, he said, "Your driver's license and vehicle registration, sir?"

"Sure," Quint said and reached across to the glove compartment to get out the registration, trying not to disturb the parole papers under which it rested. He quickly snapped the compartment and handed the trooper the registration. Then he took out his wallet and slipped his driver's license out.

"Long way from home, aren't you?" the cop asked as he flashed his light on the registration.

"Yes, sir," Quint said as he held his license and pushed his wallet back in his pocket.

"Where're you heading?"

"California." He looked at the squad cars, then back at the man. "What's going on?"

"Actually, we're looking for a woman."

Quint barely stopped his right hand from closing around the driver's license and crushing it. "A woman?"

The man returned Quint's registration and license, then he reached into the pocket of his uniform, took out a picture and handed it to him. The cop aimed the beam of his flashlight at the photo so Quint got a good look at it.

"That's her, Anne Marie Thomas."

His driver's license crushed slowly in his right hand as he stared at the head and shoulders shot, taken in full sunlight with a backdrop of what looked like a barn or stables. Quint stared at the image, at the brilliant hair tumbling in curls around a face dominated by deep green eyes and a smile that made his stomach clench.

Anne Marie Thomas was Annie and, despite her assurances to the contrary, she was indeed wanted by the police. Quint could feel a sheen of moisture on his skin, and the warm breeze was suddenly touching him with a chill that went deep into his being. "What did she do?"

"Since you aren't from around here, I doubt you've heard of the Raines family."

"No, sir, I haven't."

"Well, let's say they own most of the county and a lot of the state." He moved a bit closer and Quint thought he detected a faint look of distaste in the trooper's expression. "Their son put out a complaint on this woman."

Quint stared at the man. "What for?"

"They were supposed to get married tomorrow, but earlier this afternoon he calls the police and charges her with assault."

Quint felt as if he'd been hit himself. Annie was the runaway bride-to-be! But he couldn't comprehend the assault part. "Did you say *she* assaulted him?"

"That's right." The man actually laughed. "He's not a small guy, but she knocked him cold. And he's pressing charges. He's at our backs to find her."

Before Quint could ask any more questions or return Annie's photo to the man, another officer called out, "Hey, Joe, someone's spotted the Thomas woman back at The Amigo."

"All right," he called, then looked at Quint. "Good luck in California, sir," he said, then turned and hurried back to the nearest squad car, forgetting all about the picture.

Quint didn't move while the man got in the white car, flipped on the siren, then took off in a squeal of tires and flashing lights. When one of the other cops waved at Quint to move on, Quint looked down at the picture he still held in his hand. He pressed it flat on his thigh, catching it between the denim of his jeans and his palm.

Slowly he drove forward, through the opening in the cluster of cars, then he sped up as he hit the open road. Anne Marie Thomas. He could feel the photo still pressed against his thigh, and he grimaced. Liar. She was running because she assaulted some rich, powerful bridegroom. And he'd helped her escape from the law. An accomplice. Or an accessory. He was a paroled ex-con and he would've been a sitting duck if the cops had stopped him with her. What was probably a lover's quarrel could have landed him back in prison.

The idea of not stopping for her was very tempting, but he couldn't do it. When he'd gone half a mile and was out of sight of the roadblock, he pulled to the side of the road and turned on his flashers. Then he looked out at the dark field to his right, but couldn't see any movement.

He had some need to confront Annie with her lies, to at least tell her he knew before he left her here. And maybe to vent his feelings of being used and deceived.

He shifted in the seat and regarded the picture in the pale light of the partial moon. The image ate at him . . . the smile, the look as if she had the world by the tail. Anger welled up in him and he slapped the photo facedown on the level area of the console, then waited.

When he couldn't sit still any longer, he snatched the picture up and got out. He circled the car and leaned back against the passenger door while he stared out at the field. After what seemed an eternity, he spotted a lone figure trudging in his direction. He pushed aside an unsettling sense of relief that she'd made it and stepped into the pasture.

When Annie spotted the flashing parking lights coming through the night, she was startled that she almost felt as if she were going home. She'd made it. Quint was waiting. With everything falling apart around her, for a second she felt grounded and safe, a feeling so alien to her that she barely knew how to deal with it.

She hurried, walking faster, then she saw Quint coming toward her. He looked large and dark in the paleness of the moonlight, and he looked amazingly like a port in a storm. She walked even faster, and when she got close to Quint it seemed the most natural thing in the world for her to reach out and hold on to him.

She wrapped her arms around him, burying her face in the heat of his chest and holding on so tightly that her arms were shaking. The beating of his heart was against her cheek, and the rhythm was as fast as hers. "We made it!" she whispered in a broken voice. "Thank goodness."

Tears were close to the surface, but as his scent surrounded and filled her, mingling with his body heat, things began to shift, the way they had when she'd kissed him at the diner. A man she'd met hours ago was making her feel things that she couldn't remember ever experiencing with any other man before.

A stranger, a man she knew little about, and she had to fight the urge to hold on to him forever and never let go. She had to stop herself from moving even closer.

Then she realized something strange; Quint wasn't exactly hugging her. His hands were on her shoulders, but he was attempting to gently push her away from him. And when she looked up into his remote expression, fire burned in her cheeks. She'd reacted so intensely, and she'd been so wrong.

"You were right to avoid the roadblock. They're looking for you."

At the sound of his blunt statement, the blood drained from her face and for a second she thought she was going to pass out. "Oh, God," she breathed and reached out to Quint for support, but before she could do more than sense his heat near her fingers, he jerked back.

The action left her feeling as if she'd been hit in the stomach.

"I don't think praying's going to do you any good," he said flatly.

Then he held up a small photo in front of her, and it shook her when she recognized her own image.

"Where did you—?"

"Who is she?" he demanded in a low, rough voice.

She looked away from the photo to Quint and swallowed hard. "You know."

"No, you tell me who she is."

His tone was so cold it cut her deeply and she closed her eyes. "She's a woman who made some bad decisions in her life, then she thought she'd made one good one. She was wrong." Annie opened her eyes but didn't look at Quint. She stared at the dry brush under her sandaled feet. "She agreed to marry the wrong man, and that man wouldn't let her go."

He was silent for what seemed an eternity, then he turned away and started back to the car. She went after him and almost had to run to keep up with his long, determined stride. When they got to the car, Quint stopped so abruptly that she barely stopped herself from running into his back.

"You're on your own, Anne Marie Thomas. Your purse is under the seat and I'll get your bag out of the trunk."

His words chilled her almost as much as his actions moments ago or the fact that Trevor had the police looking for her. "Quint, the police, what did they say exactly?"

"They showed me this," he said as he held the photo out to her. "Here, it's yours."

"I don't want it. I told you, I made a mistake and—"

"You lied."

"I just thought—"

"They said you skipped out on your wedding to the son of one of the most powerful families around. Apparently, they're powerful enough to commandeer a squad of state troopers to track down the woman who assaulted their son!"

Trevor was claiming assault! She closed her eyes for a moment, almost holding her breath waiting for him to mention Sammi. "What else did the police tell you?" she asked, hating the unsteadiness in her voice.

He was silent until she opened her eyes and looked at him. "Enough to let me know I'm out of here. I don't need this kind of trouble."

She felt giddy, the world an unsteady place for her. And her need to get to Sammi was overwhelming. "Come on, just take me to the next town, then I'll leave you alone," she said and tried to step around him to go to the passenger door.

But Quint grabbed her upper arm and stopped her in her tracks. The contact was tight and firm, and she stood very still, staring at the car, but not looking at Quint. "What?" she whispered.

"All I need is to have the cops coming back this way and finding you with me."

"If we get going, they won't find you," she said, her jaw clenching to keep any trembling under control. His hold hovered just this side of real pain, but Annie didn't move. "You said you'd take me to the next town."

"I lied."

"But you—"

"So, sue me . . . or hit me."

She closed her eyes so tightly that colors exploded behind her lids. "I just pushed him, and he . . . he hit his head. Please, I need the ride," she whispered. Begging was distasteful to her, yet she knew she'd do anything to get to Sammi. "You can see what I'm up against. The Raineses have all the advantages. I don't have anything . . . including my car."

He released her unexpectedly, and Annie slowly turned to face him. "How in the hell could you assault a man?"

"I didn't. I told you, I just pushed him. He . . . he was drunk and . . ." She shrugged sharply. "He fell."

"Why does he want you back so badly?"

She shrugged, catching at a partial truth. "Trevor hates to lose. He gets what he wants, and he just happens to want me." She looked past him at the dark road. "Can we drive while we talk?"

She braced herself for more argument, but Quint surprised her when he turned and circled the car to the driver's side and got in. When he turned on the engine, Annie didn't wait for an invitation. She opened the door, scrambled in and, as the Corvette moved onto the road, she said a silent prayer of thanks that Quint hadn't tossed her out and driven away.

Quint eased the car up to sixty miles per hour, then settled back in his seat. "Why did you lie to me?" he asked abruptly.

"I didn't know you, and I didn't know if you knew the Raines family." That was the truth. "It just seemed easier if you weren't too involved. So I fudged a bit."

His snort of laughter held no humor. "What else did you 'fudge' about?"

She settled down in the seat and rested her head against the back. As long as the police hadn't mentioned Sammi, she felt as if she stood a chance. "I told you, I didn't want you to get too involved."

"That's a joke. I think I passed involved a long way back."

Quint drove in silence for a few minutes, the tension between them almost palpable.

Finally, Annie felt compelled to tell her side of things. "You asked who the woman in the photo really is. She's Anne Marie Thomas and she's from Taos, New Mexico. She was born in Arizona, moved around a lot and finally settled in Taos four years ago. She's been on her own since she was a teenager, and she worked as the manager of a small, elegant restaurant called The Place, for three years.

"She met Trevor Raines a few years ago and was momentarily dazzled by him. Then they lost touch. He came back into her life a couple of months ago. He asked her to come to Oklahoma to meet his family, then he asked her to marry him."

"You sound as if you're describing someone else's life," he said. His statement was close to the truth, especially now.

"It's mine," she said on a sigh. "My life in a nutshell."

"So, what did you overhear that made you assault this wonderful man?"

She gave him half of the truth. "I found out he didn't think marriage meant commitment."

"He was playing around?"

"Was, is, and always will," she muttered. She could feel Quint looking at her.

"I pushed him and he fell, that's all." She shifted in the seat. Now that the tension between them seemed to be easing a bit, a troubling thought came to her for the first time. "Are you married?"

"I told you how I feel about questions."

"It's a simple question. Are you married?"

"No."

"Ever married?"

"Not even close."

"One more question?"

He cast her a slanting look, then glanced back at the road. "Sure, go for it."

"What do you do for a living?"

"I'm not the son of wealthy parents, that's for sure. I've done a lot of things to make a living."

"Where are you from?"

"That's another question."

"I'm not good at math," she said.

"I was born in Florida but left there when I was a kid. The last place I lived was back east."

"And you're going to . . . ?"

"California."

"I've never been there," she said as she shifted lower in the seat.

"I was there years ago, out in Santa Barbara north of Los Angeles visiting my brother."

"Why go back?"

"It's a place to go."

She looked up at the starry sky skittering by overhead. "A place to go," she echoed, wondering if she and Sammi should head west to California. There were a lot of people there, a lot of places to get lost where the Raines family couldn't find her.

The sound of a distant siren cut through her thoughts and she bolted up, twisting to look behind them down the road. Her heart was pounding, but there were no lights in the night and the sound of the siren died out until there was just the rushing air and the sounds of the night.

"They aren't back there ... yet," Quint said.

Annie sank back down in the seat and looked ahead of them. "But they will be. Trevor won't give up. He can't." She hugged her arms around herself and rubbed the flats of her hands on her upper arms.

"He's charging you with assault."

"That's what you said."

"What are you going to do if they catch up with you?"

"I won't let that happen," she said.

"But if it does?"

She shook her head. "I'll deal with it." That's what she'd always done, including having Sammi and caring for her. "How far can the next town be?" she breathed, then as if the answer came on cue, a sign was caught in the headlights of the car.

Quint didn't look at Annie as he slowed and read the sign by the road. Jarvis 41 miles. He knew that looking at Annie only made things more complicated, the way touching her did. "Forty-one miles to civilization," he said.

"If you can call it that," Annie said. "It's so deserted out here, it almost seems like another planet."

Quint had felt that way since exiting the prison gates. Life went in a higher gear than he was used to, and it made him feel out of step. It was odd how his time with Annie could have almost been a delusion, a passing dream. Maybe he'd wake up and find himself in the four-man cell with the smell of human beings and disinfectant in the air.

Or maybe this was the first time reality had set in. He wasn't at all sure. When Annie shifted in the seat by him and the warm air was touched by that flowery scent he associated with her, reality hit him on every level. He'd had to fight himself to keep from holding on to her in the field, and now he had to fight the urge to look at her again.

Chapter Six

Quint barely covered a yawn and glanced at the clock. Midnight. He'd slept outside since he left prison, finding secluded places off the road and staying in the car with the top down. With the stars and moon overhead, he could breathe and relax, and he usually woke at first light. Today, he'd been driving since dawn, and weariness was beginning to take its toll.

"Do you want me to drive until we get to Jarvis?" Annie asked.

"No," he said immediately. Then he softened his rejection just a bit. "No one drives this car, but me."

"Is that another rule, no personal questions, no one driving the car?"

"I guess so."

"Any others?"

Not getting involved, he thought, and knew how irrevocably he'd shattered that rule with Annie. "I'm not sure."

"Well, I've got a rule about being in a car with someone who's going to fall asleep at the wheel."

Fields stretched out on both sides and as far ahead as he could see. "I'll find someplace to pull over," he said, "I only need a few hours of sleep, then we can go on to Jarvis."

"We don't need to stop," she said quickly. "That's not what I meant."

He could feel her restlessness at sitting still for very long. This assault charge had to have her more spooked than she'd admitted to him. And Trevor sounded like a man possessed. In a measure, he could understand it. If a man got involved with Annie, it wouldn't be easy to walk away. He was living proof of that.

"I need to stop," he said as the night began to blur in front of his eyes.

"But I can't—"

"I'm stopping. You're right that I'm not fit to drive much farther. There," he said, pointing in the dark shadows to trees clustered near the road to the right.

"We can't just stop by the road. What if the police—"

"No problem," he said as he slowed and eased the car onto the shoulder, then he carefully drove toward the trees. The rough ground bounced the suspension, but the field was actually fairly level. He drove to the side of the trees and saw that there was no way to drive into them. They were growing too tightly together, but it was clear on the back side, so he drove the car behind the trees and out of sight of the road.

He turned off the car and the night seemed to surround them. "They can't see us from the road, and it's quiet." He could feel Annie's nervousness. "Look, by now they know you left The Amigo in my car, and I think stopping where we can't be seen can be good. If they come this way looking for you, they'll go right on past. And if they don't come this way, you don't have a thing to worry about."

Quint adjusted his seat until it was comfortable, then he lay back. As he settled, he glanced at Annie. "Come on. Rest. You've got to be running on raw nerves. Take it easy, and we'll be on our way in a couple of hours."

He closed his eyes and tried to shut out the sensation of Annie's nearness. If he had a sleeping bag or bedroll he would have gotten out of the car and slept under the trees to put some distance between himself and Annie. But he didn't have that option. That thought almost brought a laugh. When had he had an option with this woman? Never. And that idea was as unsettling as her close presence.

Annie watched Quint and within minutes she could tell he was sound asleep. She envied him. She'd napped earlier while he drove, but right now sleep was elusive. She reached for the handle, eased the door open and quietly got out of the car. She walked toward the nearest tree and sank down on a patch of meadow grass.

She looked back at the car. It blended with the night, dark and sleek, a reflection of the man driving it. Turning from the sight, she pulled her legs up to her chest and hugged her arms around them. As she rested her chin on her bent knees, she thought about fate and how her life had been shaken up.

In twelve hours everything had changed. There was no marriage, no father for Sammi, no life that would be grounded and rooted for the child. Instead of being in her beat-up old car heading west, she was on the lam from the police, spending the night in a sleek black Corvette with a stranger who probably wanted to see the last of her as badly as she wanted to get to her daughter.

That thought brought back some of the tension and she looked back at the car. What if she fell asleep and Quint woke up and decided to leave her here? He'd wanted to see the end of her often enough. She wouldn't blame him if he took off, but she couldn't take that chance.

She scrambled to her feet, swiped at the clinging grass on her jeans, then went back to the car. As quietly as she could, she slipped into the passenger seat and shut the door. She wasn't going to make it easy for him to leave. She couldn't afford to.

She found the adjustment on the seat, eased it back and stretched out her legs, then looked toward Quint, his profile blurred in the darkness. When she finally closed her eyes, she tried to relax, but she couldn't shake the need to keep an eye open for trouble.

Gradually, though, Annie began to relax. Weariness seemed to invade her, and she slid into the softness of sleep. Her last waking thought was gratitude that she wasn't alone.

The dream came slowly out of the comforting nothingness and if she'd been awake, she would have fought against it. But in sleep anything could happen, and it did. She found herself drawn into a blurred world where all the sharp edges were gone, where pain and uncertainty hovered on the fringes, lost in the shadows.

Annie was in the car with Quint, driving through the night, slipping past the darkness together and heading for a nameless place where she knew they both belonged. It was ahead of her, rich with colors and newness, a place where she could turn to Quint, touch his face and know that he wanted her.

A place where he framed her face with his heat and strength, where no barriers existed. A place where his lips found hers, where his taste filled her and where his arms pulled her against him. A place of forgetfulness, a place where life was right.

Annie reached out, losing herself in Quint, in his scent, in his warmth, in his touch, and she knew a happiness that defied all reason. For one heartbeat, her life was perfect, then it shattered just as quickly as it had formed.

"Anne Marie!"

The sound of Trevor's voice cut through everything, and Annie saw him coming at her. When he was right in front of her, she saw that he wasn't alone. Sammi was with him, her green eyes filled with tears, her blond hair framing a pale face. "Mommy!" she sobbed. "Mommy, Mommy!"

Annie reached for her, but her hand closed on nothingness, and Trevor laughed, a horribly obscene sound. "Get out of here, Anne Marie," he said. "Just leave. I've got what I want."

"No, please, no," Annie begged as she lunged toward Trevor. But he was fading away, taking Sammi with him. All Annie could see in the blackness was her daughter's face filled with fear and she could hear Trevor's laughter.

"No! Sammi!" she screamed.

Quint had been yanked awake by screams in the night more times than he wanted to remember. But this time it wasn't some inmate having nightmares or a man ready to cause trouble. This time it was a woman, the words cutting through the night, and in a single heartbeat, he knew it was Annie.

Her scream echoed in him. "No! Sammi, no!" and Quint was instantly awake. He sat up, twisted and saw Annie in the seat by him, her hands reaching out in front of her. But her eyes were closed and her face was twisted with distress and streaked with tears. He reached out to her.

In less than a heartbeat, he had her in his arms. "No, no," she moaned and pressed her face into his shirt, her hands caught between their bodies against his chest.

He held her as closely as he could with the low console between them, and he stroked her silky hair. "It's all right. It's me, Quint. You were dreaming."

She slowly shook her head, rubbing her forehead back and forth on his chest. "A dream," she sobbed in relief. "It was only a dream."

"Yes, just a dream," he whispered, his fingers tangling in her hair as he closed his eyes. Her fear was a living thing, with an intensity that was almost painful for him to witness. "It's over."

She was very still, then slowly she moved back enough for him to look down into her tear-stained face. When he met the full impact of her gaze in the pale moonlight, he knew how horribly unaltruistic his actions were. He'd wanted to hold her from the first, he'd wanted to feel her close, to have her heat and sweetness right here. When her tongue darted out to touch her softly parted lips, he knew what else he wanted. And wanted desperately.

Slowly he lowered his head to hers, and when his lips found hers, emotions that felt as if they had been in their own prison exploded into freedom. He tasted the saltiness of tears as her lips parted. And Quint gave in to every need that bombarded him. All that mattered was the reality of this woman and a hunger in him that had a life of its own.

He could feel her straining toward him, her breasts crushing against his chest as her arms slipped around his waist. Her essence seemed to permeate him, gliding into his being, filtering into his soul. When she worked her hands under his shirt, he groaned at the skin-on-skin contact, and he needed to touch her as well as feel her touch.

He fumbled with her shirt, somehow working her buttons open, and the cotton slipped off her shoulders. He tasted the heat of her throat, the softness of her hair brushing his face, and his hands skimmed over her naked shoulders. His body tightened, and the aching need for her grew with breathtaking speed.

He moved his hand lower and the covering of an ornate bra was the only barrier left. As he tasted her, searching her mouth, running his tongue over her teeth, he found a row of buttons at the back of the bra that ran down to her waist. The tiny silk-covered fasteners felt as if they had fabric loops around them, and his fingers were awkward in his haste to banish all barriers between them.

He felt her move, shifting back enough to look at him, and he couldn't take his eyes off her. Her moon-shadowed eyes were heavy with desire that echoed in him. The cotton of her shirt had fallen off her shoulders, and the lace-and-satin bodice provocatively contained her breasts. Yet it revealed enough of the swelling softness above the lace to seductively tantalize every nerve ending in him.

He touched her with the tips of his fingers, tracing the swelling of her breast and feeling the beating of her heart. The ache grew in him, the agony of wanting her with a surety that almost took his breath away.

"Quint," she breathed, his name on the softness of the warm night stark contrast to the scream of fear before.

As his finger dipped to the cleavage, to tuck under the lacy cover, he suddenly remembered her scream that had torn him from sleep. His finger stilled. *No, Sammy, no.*

It wrenched at him when he realized she'd been screaming for a man, and not her ex-fiancé. A chill began to rob him of the fire, and he drew back. She was running away from one man to another, and he'd let himself get caught in the middle.

Even the sight of her softness, her parted lips, her hands on him, wasn't enough for him to forget. And he wished it was. He wished he could block out her cries, pretend they'd never happened. But he couldn't.

He drew back from her, exhaling a shaky breath, then he gripped the steering wheel with both hands. The leather was a poor substitute for the feel of her, but it kept him centered. "Bad dreams cause stupid reactions," he muttered.

"Quint?" she whispered, but he didn't look at her.

"Tell me something?" he said, staring at the dark hulk of the spreading trees near the car.

"What?"

"What was your dream about?"

He heard her take a shuddering breath. "I . . . it's nerves, all this trouble . . . I . . ."

He didn't look at her again. Instead, he turned the key and started the car. "It's almost four o'clock.

Dawn's going to be here in a few hours, and it's time to get out of here and head for Jarvis.'' And time to bring this madness to a screeching halt.

Annie sank into the warm leather, a strange shakiness deep inside her. To respond to a man like that, to a man she barely knew, was frightening. She wrapped her arms around herself and lifted her face, letting the warm air brush her skin. What had happened with Quint went beyond a mere response. She knew that if he hadn't drawn back, she wouldn't have stopped herself.

She bit her lip hard. The idea that she hadn't wanted their embraces to stop was stark and painful. Was she crazy? She'd made such mistakes because of being impulsive, and this was certainly impulsive. Or was she that needy? Did she have to have someone there for her? She never would have thought that answer could be yes before... until now.

She didn't need anyone else. She couldn't. There had to be just her and Sammi now.

"A question?" Quint said, his voice rough in the night.

She didn't look at him, not when just the sound of his voice could set her nerves on edge. "What?"

"Why were you going to marry Raines?"

She rested her head against the seat back and closed her eyes. "I thought I should," she said with real honesty.

"Thought you should?"

She knew that sounded odd, but she wasn't about to tell him about Sammi. The man could barely deal with the police and Trevor coming after her. "I mean, it seemed right. I told you we knew each other a few years ago, then he came back and he said that he loved me, that he wanted to get married.'' She could barely say the words, words that had been a blatant lie. ''I came out to meet his family, and he asked me again.''

''And you agreed?''

''Yes.''

''I don't suppose it hurt that his family has tons of money.''

She heard the edge in his voice and it hurt. ''I didn't know that, not until I got here.''

''And that's when you said yes to his proposal.''

''Listen, it's not—''

''As if you were passionately in love?'' he cut her off.

''What?'' she asked, turning to look at him and wishing she hadn't.

The moonlight touched the planes and angles of his face, and the sight of him took her breath away.

''Love, passion. Obviously you didn't delude yourself to that extent.''

She didn't know why his words stung so much. ''How can you say that?''

''You don't deck someone you love. Then you walked out...or at least, ran out, didn't you?''

She wished she could say that wasn't the way it had been with Trevor, but she knew it came very close to the truth. But she wanted everything for Sammi, not herself. ''I left. Period.''

''He was playing around?''

She took an unsteady breath. ''That was part of it.''

''What else is there?''

Another part of truth came from her. ''I was going to marry him, but I overheard him telling a friend about some girl, and then he told him that he was only marrying me so he wouldn't get kicked out by his parents."

"Why would his parents kick him out?"

"He'd been in trouble off and on, and I think his parents thought if he got married he'd become responsible and settle down."

"So he went looking for a bride?"

"I guess so." She flinched when Quint laughed, the sound jarring to her. "It's not funny," she muttered.

"Damn straight it isn't funny. You didn't know a thing about it when you agreed to marry him?"

"No. I believed him."

"What did he believe about you?"

"Pardon me?"

"What did you tell him? That you loved him?"

It startled Annie to think that she'd never said those words to Trevor... or to any other person in her life except for Sammi. "I guess he assumed that I did."

"If you agreed to marriage, it's a good bet he assumed it."

She knew getting married and having the child as his pawn so he could have access to his family funds was all he'd thought about. "I couldn't go through with it."

"When you found out the reasons he wanted to marry you, you got into a fight?"

"I confronted him. He was drunk and he said things that were...upsetting, then he tried to..." She bit her lip hard and veered back to the truth Quint already knew. "He was afraid that he was going to lose his family fortune, that he'd have to get an honest job and work like the rest of us."

"That's why he's going after you?"

"He's mad and probably a bit desperate," she said truthfully. "His folks will think he fouled things up again." She looked ahead of them. "Quint?"

"Yeah?"

"I appreciate all of this, I really do. You could have kept driving after the roadblock when you found out about the assault thing."

"I almost did."

His blunt words made her breath catch. "You did?"

"I told you I don't want to get involved, and if this ex-fiancé has so much money and power behind him, he could make things pretty tight for both of us."

"Not you. You didn't do a thing. I'd just tell him you gave me a ride."

"Maybe he'll think you were running away from him to be with me?"

"Oh, I don't think so."

"It sounds logical to me. You walked out on him to go to another man."

He was right. It sounded logical, but another man wasn't even in the picture. "Trevor wouldn't think that. He's probably certain that no man could compete with him."

"Or with his money."

"He probably thinks that, too."

"This friend you're going to meet in New Mexico—"

She cut him off. She couldn't keep talking about this and not trip herself up. So she changed the subject. "Have you been in Oklahoma before?"

He looked at her. "You aren't going to tell me, are you?"

"I'm just tired of talking about this."

He fingered the steering wheel. "All right. I was in Oklahoma once years ago."

"You lived around here?"

"No, I worked near Tulsa."

"Doing what?"

"I was a bodyguard."

She stared at him. He had the size and the bearing. She had seen him take out Bugsy with one kick. Yet she remembered the gentleness in him when she'd come out of the nightmare. "Are you serious?"

"Dead serious."

"Who were you working for?"

"A businessman who had enemies."

"How long did you work for him?"

"Until he died."

She stared at him. "He was murdered?"

He cast her a darkly shadowed look, but she could see the hint of a smile tug at his lips. "He died of a heart attack, not a bullet or a bomb. And I wasn't anywhere near him when he keeled over and bit the big one."

She sank back in the seat. "Have you worked for anyone famous?"

"A few, here and there," he murmured.

"Who?"

He looked at her again. "A couple of singers."

"Really? Who?"

"Have you ever heard of Bentley Days?"

Who hadn't heard of the soul singer? "You worked for him? You're kidding?"

"I wish I was. He was a royal pain in the butt."

"How long did you work for him?"

"Until I couldn't take it anymore, about a year and a half."

"What did he do?"

"He wouldn't do anything I asked. He wasn't about to alter his life-style to stay alive, so I finally walked."

"Where did you go?"

"To another job. Then another."

"Are you working for anyone now?"

He was silent and she thought at first that he hadn't heard the question. But just when she was about to repeat it, he said, "No. I'm changing professions."

"What are you going to do now?"

"I haven't decided, but it's not going to be body-guarding. I think those days are over."

"That's too bad."

"No, it's a relief."

"You said your brother lives in California."

"No, I didn't."

"Yes you did, when you were talking about going to Santa Barbara."

"Oh, yeah. I guess I did. Actually, I think I'll hit Patrick up for a job. He owns his own paint and body shop."

"That sounds tame after being a bodyguard."

"Tame isn't all bad." He motioned ahead of them. "Maybe that's Jarvis."

She looked and saw the glow of lights in the pre-dawn sky, partially hidden by low hills. She wanted to get to Sammi, but for some reason the idea of leaving Quint made her feel uneasy. And vulnerable. He'd been a bodyguard of sorts for her over the past hours. "It could be."

"Where do you want to go when we get there?"

"The bus station, I think. I'll get the first bus west, then get off along the line and find a rental car." She sighed. "I hate doing this, but I can't let Trevor find me, and now that he's gone to the police…'' Her voice trailed off, then she took a breath. ''I'm sure not going to let him put me in jail for pushing him when he was … being such a jerk.''

''He doesn't have a clue where you're going?''

There were so many things she hadn't thought out. Of course he'd know where she was going, and he could be there waiting for her when she arrived at Jeannie's. ''Yes, I guess he'd figure it out.''

''Then don't go to New Mexico. Change your plans and go someplace he'd never think to look for you.''

''I have to go there first,'' she said.

''To meet your friend?''

''Yes.'' But she couldn't meet Jeannie at her home or the restaurant. She'd have to call her when she got to the bus station and make plans where to meet.

''I figured as much,'' he muttered.

Chapter Seven

Annie didn't have a clue why Quint sounded so put out by her simple statements, and she didn't have time to worry about it when they neared the outskirts of Jarvis.

She was surprised Jarvis wasn't a tiny town like Scarlet. It sprawled out in either direction toward low hills. It was an assortment of buildings, both houses and businesses, that were low to the ground with flat roofs and a few trees shading the wide streets.

Right under the sign welcoming everyone to Jarvis, population 35,000, was a sign that listed the bus terminal as one mile and an arrow pointing south. Before she could say anything to Quint, he saw the same sign and turned south on the next street.

They drove down the deserted street, past closed businesses with false Western fronts, then Annie spotted a blue-and-white neon sign. It was off to the right just beyond a hardware store and in front of an old building with a flat roof, peeling paint on the walls, and a jutting portico out in front where a single bus idled near the glass entry doors.

Quint drove past the front under old-fashioned streetlights and turned right into a parking lot to the side of the building that held a handful of cars. He didn't bother parking the Corvette, but stopped near the entry, let the car idle, and he turned to Annie. "I guess this is it."

Annie held her purse to her middle and looked at Quint. "I don't know how to thank you for what you've done for me."

He actually smiled at her, a slow, devastating smile that made her eyes burn with the sting of tears. "Did I have a choice?"

"Yes," she whispered. "You did."

He shifted toward her and, without warning, touched her cheek with the tips of his fingers. The heat sizzled through her, and she was afraid to move. Afraid to break the contact, but afraid if she didn't, she'd reach out to him one last time. "I actually don't think I did," he said in a rough whisper.

She closed her eyes tightly for a moment, then took a shaky breath before looking at Quint again. For a long moment she stared at him, memorizing every detail of the man. Then his fingers trailed down her cheek, and the contact was broken. "I won't forget what you did," she said in a tight voice she barely recognized as her own.

For a second the world seemed to stop, then Quint leaned toward her and brushed his lips against her forehead. "I hope you get where you want to go, Anne Marie Thomas," he whispered. He drew back and turned from her. "I'll get your bag out of the back."

Annie took a second to inhale one deep breath, catching at the lingering scents in the car mellowness of leather and a certain essence that seemed to be all Quint. She stored it all away with the other memories, then opened the door and got out.

She turned and Quint was there with her bag. "Do you want me to take it inside for you?" he asked.

She shook her head. "No, thanks." She didn't want to draw this out any longer than she had to. When he passed her the bag, she made very sure not to touch him in the process, then she had her heavy bag in one hand, her purse in the other.

She looked up at Quint, marvelling at how short a time she'd known him and how sad she felt knowing she would never see him again. Without trusting herself to say anything else, she headed away from him and went toward the entry to the terminal. When she passed the idling bus and went up the single step to the glass doors, she had to fight an urge to take one last look at Quint.

Instead, she pushed the closest door open with her shoulder and went inside.

Quint watched Annie disappear and knew it was safer this way. She was going to her "friend" and he was getting on with a life that had taken a short, but temporary detour. He turned, closed the trunk, then went around, got back in the car and put it in gear.

As he drove toward the far end of the lot, he repeated a mistake he'd made the first time he left Annie. He took one last look in the rearview mirror. This time he didn't see Annie at all, but he saw flashing lights and he hit the brakes.

He twisted in the seat and saw two squad cars pulling into the drive by the entry. One stopped behind the idling bus, the other one went around and parked nose into the curb in front of the bus, effectively blocking it from leaving.

When the cop in the front car got out, Quint saw him clearly for a moment, and he knew right then they were after Annie. The man was the one who had talked to Quint at the roadblock and showed him Annie's picture. Trevor Raines really meant business and wasn't giving up. Worse yet, Annie was in there, a sitting duck without any idea about what was going to happen.

At that moment, Quint gave up even trying to rationalize anything he did where Annie was concerned. Instead of driving out onto the street and leaving only his dust behind, he went to the back of the asphalt lot and parked the Corvette out of sight behind a group of trash bins.

He got out, looked around and when he spotted a side entrance, he headed for it. With any luck the door wouldn't be locked from the inside. He went up the single step, grabbed the handle and the door opened without a sound. He stepped into what looked like a locker room, where cool air brushed across his skin as he looked around the gray-and-green space. Worn tiles were underfoot and gray metal lockers lined the walls on either side.

He crossed to an opening directly opposite the side entry and looked into the main room that smelled of age and cigarette smoke. A low ceiling umbrellaed an area with benches in the middle, more lockers on the wall by Quint and a ticket counter and luggage area on the far wall.

Maybe half a dozen passengers were waiting in the room, a couple stretched out on the hard wooden benches sleeping, the others scattered around, reading or just staring off into space. Quint barely had time to see that Annie was nowhere in sight before the front door opened and two cops strode in.

Quickly Quint ducked back to use the side of the nearest lockers as partial shelter, and he watched the two men cross to the ticket counter. His heart hammered against his ribs; the cop who knew him was less than thirty feet from him at the ticket counter.

Where was Annie? She couldn't have left by the front door without running into the cops, and she certainly didn't duck out the side door. He looked across the room, but the only doors were at the back where the luggage went. Then he looked to his left past a series of vending machines and he spotted restrooms; that was the only place she could be if she was still in the building.

He made sure the cop still had his back to him as he spoke to the ticket agent, then, as casually as he could, he stepped out into the main room. When he ducked into the alcove, he paused self-consciously before the door to the ladies' room, astonished at how far he would go to keep Annie from being locked up, then pushed the door back and eased inside.

He found himself in a narrow room with a sagging sofa against one wall with a mottled mirror over it, and double-stacked lockers on the facing wall. Double doors at the far end were closed, and he couldn't hear anything except the low drone of elevator music being piped in from the waiting room.

No one was in here and, for a moment, he had the thought that maybe Annie wasn't here because Annie didn't exist. He'd produced her from an imagination that had grown too active in prison, an imagination that had drawn him into the Oklahoma night, into a ladies' room in a run-down bus terminal, looking for a woman who'd turned his world on its ear and jeopardized his freedom.

But as he turned to get the hell out while he still could, he spotted her suitcase pushed between the wall and the end of the couch. Just as he started toward it to make sure it was real, the double doors to his right swung open and he turned.

Annie was there, staring at him as if he were a ghost.

"Quint?" she whispered as she slowly crossed to where he stood. "What...what are you doing here?"

He didn't have an answer for that. He wished he did, but nothing made sense about what he was doing. Not any more than it made sense that without even touching her, he could remember the feel of her as if the contact had just taken place. He jammed his fingertips in the pockets of his jeans and spoke quickly, hoping to grab at some form of sanity.

"The cops are out there looking for you."

Annie could feel the blood draining from her face at an alarming rate. Seeing Quint there had startled her. She'd never expected to see him again, and for a split second she knew such relief and pleasure at the sight of him that everything else had faded.

Then he told her the situation and reality hit her with a sickening blow. "What?" she managed.

"The trooper who showed me your picture at the roadblock is out there talking to the ticket agent right now."

"Damn it," she said as she turned from Quint. She hugged her arm around herself as she faced her own reflection in the distorted mirror on the wall. She looked as if she were hugging herself to try and hold herself together, and that was truer than she cared to admit.

"They're hell-bent on getting you."

"This is all like a nightmare that won't stop even when I'm awake," she said.

"Well, the nightmare's going to get very real in the next minute or two if we don't get out of here and get out fast."

She looped her purse over her shoulder, then moved over to grab her suitcase. With a grip on the heavy bag, she turned and hurried past Quint toward the door. "Let's go," she said over her shoulder.

Quint startled her when he touched her shoulder. When she turned, he let her go to reach past her and open the door just enough to see out into the terminal.

"There he is," Quint whispered so close to her ear that she felt the heat of his breath ruffle her hair.

She stared out the opening and tightened when she saw a uniformed trooper across the waiting room. Right then another ticket agent came up behind the desk, and the trooper handed her something. As the agent took it and studied it, Quint drew back and let the door swing shut.

Annie turned and Quint was halfway across the room heading to the double doors that led into the toilet area. "Wait right there," he said as he went through the doors and disappeared. But he wasn't gone more than a few seconds before he came back out. "The window's too small to get through," he said, then without missing a beat, he was right in front of her. "We've only got one chance."

She didn't get an opportunity to ask what it was before he said, "Just follow me and keep quiet." He cracked the door again, looked out, then turned back to her and unexpectedly reached for her hand. As his fingers closed around her hand, he drew her with him out the door.

Annie caught sight of the cop at the desk with his back to them for a fraction of a second, then Quint was taking her straight across from the ladies' room to the men's room. The next thing she knew they were inside and the door was closing behind them.

There was no lounge in here, just one long, narrow room with urinals and only two of the six stalls had doors on them. "Hey?" Quint called and his voice echoed around them.

When no one answered, he hurried with her to the last stall and pushed back the swinging door.

"Quint," she breathed, "we can't—"

He didn't stop. He pulled her into the stall with him, closed the door and threw the bolt. Then he turned to Annie, let go of her hand and pressed one finger to her lips. "If you want to get out of this without going to jail or being forced back to Trevor, just do as I say. Trust me."

She looked into his dark eyes and didn't even hesitate. "What do you want me to do?"

He took her suitcase out of her hand, put it on the top of the tank on the toilet, then put her purse on top of that. He dropped the lid on the toilet, sat down on it and the next thing Annie knew, he pulled her down onto his lap. He shifted, putting his arm around her waist, then whispered near her ear, "If the door opens, pull your feet up. Don't move and don't make a sound."

She closed her eyes, feeling as if she were being bombarded by sensations—the heat of his breath on her cheek, the feeling of his arm around her waist, the casual way his other arm rested across her thighs.

"This is crazy," she whispered, and knew that about covered everything that was happening, and not just her hiding in a men's room.

"Amen." Quint's soft word lingered in the air, and she could feel his racing heart against her arm caught between their bodies. Despite his quick thinking and his apparent coolness under pressure, he wasn't exactly taking this lightly.

When she opened her eyes, she met his midnight dark scrutiny and her breath caught in her chest. And when his gaze slowly fell to her lips, she couldn't breathe at all. Even under these absurd, dangerous circumstances, this man had the ability to narrow the world to just the two of them, with a mere look.

Whatever spell he was weaving was shattered when a door slammed against a nearby wall, and the muffled sound of voices could be heard at a distance. Quint touched her parted lips with his finger. "Shh," he whispered and his hold around her waist tightened.

A moment later the door to the men's room flew open so hard that the metal barrier hit the cement block wall with a vibrating thud. Quint shifted, slipped his arm under Annie's legs and helped her lift them up out of sight.

"Go in and check," a man said, his voice echoing in the room. "That last woman was sure she saw her come over this way."

"Maybe she saw someone else, or maybe the Thomas woman went out the side door and kept going in that black Corvette."

Annie felt Quint's arm spasm slightly and tighten around her waist even more.

"Yeah, maybe, but I hate to think the dame could slip past us and disappear like Houdini."

"Yeah. Let me take a look in here," one of the men said, then footsteps struck the gray tiles. "Hello?" he called out, then something struck their stall door. "Hey, someone in there?"

"There's more stalls," Quint called out in a voice he'd altered with a slight twang. "Take your choice. I'm busy."

"I just wanted to ask if you've seen anyone else coming in here?"

"This ain't exactly a team sport," Quint snapped.

"Well, did you hear anyone come in here in the past few minutes?"

"I wasn't checking the traffic, but I heard the door open and close. No one came in."

"Did you see anyone by the phones when you came in? A woman with red hair, in her midtwenties, pretty, in blue jeans and a white shirt?"

Quint looked right at Annie. "What're you asking for?"

"Listen man, I'm a state trooper. I'm asking nice if you saw a woman like that?"

Quint didn't hesitate. "Nope. Sure didn't."

"Damn," the cop muttered.

"You got a problem?" Quint asked without looking away from Annie.

"Yeah, you could say that," the cop said.

Annie held her breath when she heard the man walking away, then he spoke to someone else. "She must have made it out the side door."

"Yeah, that's what it looks like . . ."

The other man's words trailed off as they rushed out, the door clicking shut behind them. As soon as the room was quiet again, Annie would have scrambled off of Quint's lap to get out of there, but his hold on her tightened. She turned to look at him. "We have to—"

"Shh," he whispered. "Sit tight. They might come back or be waiting outside. Give them a few minutes, then I'll go and check to see if they left."

Annie looked at Quint, into the dark intensity of his expression, and a certain sense of the ridiculous surfaced, fighting past the fear and uneasiness. She was in the men's bathroom, sitting on the lap of a man she barely knew, in a toilet stall, trying to evade the police.

It shocked her that hysterical laughter was so close to the surface, but it was there, and she had to clap her hand over her mouth to try to stifle it. But even closing her eyes couldn't stop the tears that began to run down her cheek.

"Hey, they're probably gone," Quint said in a low whisper by her ear.

When she opened her eyes, the laughter was gone as suddenly as it had come. But the tears didn't stop. Noiseless sobs all but choked her, and she pressed her face into Quint's shoulder while she cried silently. When he brushed her hair with a gentle motion, skimming over her small cut, something in her began to relax, and she released a shuddering breath.

"Oh, I'm sorry," she mumbled, but didn't move away from Quint.

"You've been through hell. You've got a right," he said, his voice a rough rumble against her cheek. "Get it out of your system."

His words stopped any more tears as she suddenly thought that crying was one thing, but sitting here with him like this was something entirely different. When his fingers touched her chin and tipped her face up until she had to look into his eyes, everything changed. His gaze was intense, a fire deep in his eyes that was beginning to flare to life in Annie, and it scared her almost as much as the police had moments ago.

When Quint exhaled, Annie could feel the world start to narrow to just the two of them again. But the spell wasn't broken this time. It grew and pulled her in until the feeling of being held in Quint's arms was everything. The desire to kiss him was so potent, and nothing had ever seemed as natural to Annie as lifting her face to him.

The kiss was deep and searching, with a passion in it that flamed white hot almost instantly. The stunning intensity of the contact shattered every piece of logic, every thread of reason, and Annie wrapped her arms around Quint's neck. She buried her fingers in his thick hair, catching at the taste of the man, and inviting his tender invasion.

She had no idea where this was going, but she knew that despite the circumstances, she was glad Quint came back. That he was here with her, holding her, touching her, exploring her, and the rightness of it had nothing to do with logic. When his hand found her breast, she strained against his touch, an ache deep inside her building quickly.

Then the sound of the outer door crashing open again shattered the moment. Annie jerked back and Quint stared at her, his eyes burning with the same need she knew was in her own expression. A light sheen of moisture filmed his skin, and his nostrils flared with each ragged breath he took.

Annie never looked away from Quint as someone came storming into the rest room muttering under his breath.

Water ran in one of the basins, there was splashing, then whoever had come in, left. As the door clicked shut, Quint exhaled unsteadily, and when he spoke in a vaguely hoarse voice, he didn't even mention what had just happened between them.

"You need to change your clothes. The cop's giving descriptions of what you're wearing. You've got your suitcase here. Get out something else to wear."

She looked around the gray-walled stall. "Here?"

"This is it," Quint said, then eased her off his lap until she was standing on legs that were far from steady.

When he stood, she deliberately didn't let her gaze drop below his waist. She didn't have to. He looked at her intently, then reached and undid the bolt on the door as he spoke softly. "I'll stand guard outside, and if anyone comes in, get up on the seat. I'll tell them this stall doesn't work."

She looked up at Quint and had to ask one question. "Why are you doing this?"

He studied her intently for what seemed an eternity before he whispered, "I wish I knew." Then he turned and opened the door. He checked the area before he looked back at Annie. "We don't have much time, so hurry."

When he stepped out and closed the door, she sagged back against the cold metal wall. She took a deep breath, then pushed all of her confusion to one side and reached for the suitcase. She laid it on the toilet seat, opened it and took out a pair of beige shorts with pleats at the front and a soft pink blouse.

Quickly she stepped out of her sandals, slipped off her jeans and shrugged out of her shirt. She pushed the clothes into the suitcase, then tried to twist her hands behind her to undo the satin buttons on the bustier.

Quint's stomach was killing him. Nerves refused to settle and he paced back and forth in the dreary space, every sound from the stall getting his attention. Thoughts of what had happened just moments ago flooded his mind. His body tightened treacherously, threatening to display everything he was trying to fight and he fought to push the images out of his mind.

He stopped at the nearest sink, turned on the cold water, cupped it in his hands and splashed it on his face. But the action did little to kill the response his body seemed intent on having to the woman behind the gray metal door.

He grabbed at a paper towel, rubbed it roughly over his face, then wadded it into a ball and tossed it into the overflowing trash container by the door. He turned and crossed to the stall door and rapped softly on it. "Hurry up," he said in a tight whisper. "We can't waste much more time."

"I'm trying," he heard Annie mumble. "But, I..."

He pushed open the stall door and when he almost hit Annie with the barrier, he froze. She stood in front of him, her suitcase open on the closed toilet, and all she had on was a pair of beige shorts and that lace-and-satin bra thing he'd seen before.

He knew that she had to fight the urge to cross her arms over her breasts, but she didn't give in to it. She stood there and spoke in a breathy whisper, "I can't get this damn thing undone."

"Then leave it on," he said more abruptly than he intended, keeping his distance.

"Can't." She reached behind her with one hand and twisted trying to reach her back. "I've got them half undone, and I can't just—"

He felt his control starting to shatter, and he spoke quickly. "Turn around."

She stared at him.

"Turn around," he said, making himself not reach out to turn her himself. "We don't have time for this."

Chapter Eight

When Annie turned her back to him, Quint looked at the row of satin buttons that were slipped through fabric loops. Then he started to undo the tiny buttons one at a time, and made very sure he didn't touch any of the silky skin under the fine material. He managed to get them all undone, and as the fabric fell apart, he had a fleeting image of her bare back. He turned and stepped out of the stall as he muttered, "Let's get going."

He never looked back until the stall door was closed, then he stared at the gray metal before he slowly lifted his hands up in front of him. They were shaking, but that was the least of his worries when it came to this woman. He could see Annie's bare feet under the door, then she pushed her feet into her sandals.

The next thing, the door opened and she was there just doing up the buttons on a pale pink blouse. "Done," she said.

He looked at the still open suitcase behind her. "Get that thing fastened, and I'll check outside to see what's going on."

He was glad to move away, to go to the door and ease it back. The distance between himself and Annie was very welcome right now. He looked out into the waiting room and couldn't see anyone but a man sleeping on a bench in the center of the room.

"Be right back," he said over his shoulder, then went out farther, past the pay phones and got a good, unobstructed look around.

A ticket agent was working at a computer with his back to the room. The bus out front must have left, because the rest of the room was basically empty, except for the man sleeping on the bench and a woman reading a novel near the luggage area. Quint looked at the side door, then quietly walked across to it, looked through the sheet glass and saw the all but deserted parking lot. He couldn't see anything moving at all, and no trooper cars in sight.

He turned, glanced at the ticket agent who was still busy at the computer, then he went back to the alcove. Quietly he went back into the men's room. Annie was in the doorway of the stall with her suitcase in one hand and her purse clutched to her side. Her coppery hair was still in the band, but if anyone noticed anything about her, it had to be her hair.

"Have you got some sort of hat in that suitcase?" he asked without going closer.

"Just a baseball cap that I—"

"Perfect. Get it out and put it on while I keep watch." He turned without waiting for her to answer, and he held the door ajar enough to see anyone who might come in their direction.

He stared straight ahead until he heard Annie speak right behind him. "How's this?"

He turned and Annie was close to him, her hair tucked under a white cotton bill cap. And any hope that she'd look less appealing that way was shattered. If anything, she looked more lovely, with her fine bone structure exposed and her eyes looking incredibly large and green.

"It'll do," he muttered. "All right, we'll go out together. You stay between me and the wall. No matter how much you want to run, walk at an easy pace. We'll go to the side door about twenty feet down on the right. Go out the door, down the step and the car's parked behind trash bins near the back wall."

He took the car keys out of his pocket, then held it out to her. "Get in the car, get down and wait for five minutes. If I'm not out by then, or if you see the cops anywhere around, get the hell out of here."

"Quint, I can't just leave you like that."

He cupped her chin with his free hand and it unnerved him to feel she was trembling. "Annie," he said softly and urgently. "Just do what I'm asking you to do, and don't look back."

She stared at him, and he could see the glistening of tears in her eyes. The last thing he needed, and the last thing he could cope with now, was more tears. "I don't know how to thank you," she whispered.

"Don't thank me. Just do as I ask."

He let go of her chin, reached for her hand, then pressed his keys in her palm. As she closed her fingers around the keys, he turned from her. When they left this room, they were exposed. And neither one of them stood a chance if the cops were waiting out there. Annie could be locked up or taken back to Raines and he'd be taken back to prison if the truck driver he'd hit had filed assault charges against him.

There was no looking back now. Fool or savior, he wasn't quite sure what he was, but as he looked back at Annie, he knew he didn't have a choice. He'd do what he had to do to make sure she never went through a fraction of what he did being locked up, to hell with the reason she was going to New Mexico.

He reached for her suitcase and took it from her, then he opened the door, looked out and motioned for Annie to come with him. She stayed behind him until they walked out into the main terminal, then she did what he'd told her to do. She fell in step between him and the wall. They didn't touch, but Quint could literally feel her presence.

He had to force himself to walk casually and quietly, while he kept the ticket agent in sight out of the corner of his eye. When they reached the side door, he turned his back on Annie and watched the terminal. When Annie opened the door, warm air swept into the room. For a fleeting moment, he felt Annie press her hand to his back, then the contact was gone as if it had never been made.

He felt the door close, and he didn't have to turn and look to know Annie was gone. He couldn't even sense her near him anymore.

Carefully, Quint turned and when he reached for the door, he looked through the glass at the parking lot. Annie was nowhere in sight. He pushed open the door, stepped out and walked down the single step, scanning the area as he went, but he couldn't see anyone at all.

When he reached the Corvette, the car looked empty. And for a moment, his heart lurched in fear that she was gone. But as he circled to the driver's side, he glanced inside and saw her crouched down between the dash and the front seat.

He reached inside, flipped the trunk release, then went around and dropped her suitcase in the trunk. Then he went back around to the driver's side. When he glanced at Annie, her features were lost in the soft shadows, but she held out his keys to him. The metal was warm from her touch.

He got in, started the car, and easing back from the protection of the bins, he headed for the far end of the parking lot. He fully expected that at any moment, someone would come running out of the building yelling at them to stop. But as he swung onto the street, all was quiet except for the throb of the engine and some night birds.

He didn't look at Annie again until he passed the city limits of Jarvis and the town faded into the distance behind the sleek black car. He deliberately kept below the speed limit until he glanced in his mirror and only saw dark road behind them. Slowly, he pressed down on the accelerator, then he looked over at Annie, still crouched out of sight.

"Come on up and get comfortable," he said. "We're out of there, and it doesn't look as if we're being followed."

While she scrambled up and sat on the seat, Quint checked the rearview mirror. But her startled yell jarred him. He looked at her as she leaned over the seat grabbing at the white hat she'd been wearing; but she didn't stand a chance of catching it before it was whipped back and out of sight by the rushing air.

"Damn it," she muttered as she flopped down in the seat again.

"Anything that's not tied down or held down is fair game in a convertible," Quint said.

"I guess so."

He motioned to the glove compartment. "Look in there and get the map out. We've got the road to ourselves right now, but it might not be that way for long."

While Annie found the map, Quint noticed he was down to less than a quarter of a tank of gas. Enough to get them out of the area, but he'd have to stop soon.

"How in blazes—" Annie muttered and Quint glanced at her fighting the map, attempting to fold it while the rushing air was trying to snatch it out of her hands.

"Remember your hat," he said. "We don't want to lose that map."

She managed to fold it, and Quint flicked on an interior light that gave her enough illumination around her legs to read the map. "Find Jarvis," he told her.

She bent over the map as she held it against her leg, then said, "All right, I found Jarvis. Now what?"

"See if there's any road that goes south into Texas and cuts west to New Mexico."

"There's one that looks as if it's just ahead. It dips down into the panhandle, then cuts right into the north corner of New Mexico."

"Perfect. Keep your eyes open for the turn, and after we're off this road, start looking for a gas station."

"Good, I need to make a phone call," she murmured as she refolded the map. "I tried to make a call back at the bus station, but the line was busy. That's why I didn't get my ticket before you showed up."

"It probably saved your skin that the line was busy. If the call had gone through, you would have been standing there talking when the cops went inside, or you would have been at the ticket counter. Either way, they would have caught you."

"They still could have if you hadn't come in to find me. I probably would have walked right out into their arms."

Instead, she'd been in his arms. "Well, you didn't."

"No, I ended up in the men's room sitting in a stall evading the police." She sighed almost wistfully. "I'm sorry I lost it back there. It's just everything seemed so ridiculous...and scary."

Images of her sitting on his lap or standing in front of him in the stall were burned into his mind, the way the feel of her under his hands seemed to be branded on his skin. "We got out of there," he said quickly. "And we're heading west."

"Yes, we are," Annie said, and she knew that that was all she could ask for right now.

When she opened the glove compartment to put the map back, a thick white envelope fell at her feet. She picked it up, put the map back in the glove compartment, then tried to put the envelope in on top of it. But when she tried to close the glove compartment it wouldn't quite snap, so she took the envelope back out and looked at Quint, ready to ask him what to do with it.

He was facing straight ahead, his eyes on a horizon, which was starting to lighten with the coming dawn. And something in the set of his jaw stopped her from speaking.

She looked around, then remembered the way the hat was snatched out of the car by the rushing air. Not taking any chances, she pushed the thick envelope down between the seat and the console. Then she closed the glove compartment and sat back. She rested her head on the back support and spotted the sign for the secondary road.

"There it is," she said to Quint and pointed at the sign.

Without a word, he slowed the car, turned onto the road, then sped up and headed south toward Texas. Annie closed her eyes, forced her hands open on her thighs and tried to relax. When Quint stopped for gas she could call Jeannie and arrange to meet someplace other than the house or the restaurant. And soon she'd get to Sammi, then she could take off and start a whole new life.

That thought made her feel good, but at the same time, another thought came. Soon she'd really be saying goodbye to Quint. And that thought hurt, a lot more than it should have.

She twisted to the right, turning her face to the door, and she concentrated on seeing Sammi again. The next thing she knew, Quint was gently nudging her arm and interrupting a deep and dreamless sleep.

"Annie, wake up."

As Quint drew back, she sat up and rubbed at her eyes, then looked around. The sun was fully up now, and it cast a clean, bright light over a land that rolled gently off into distant foothills. Rangeland was spotted with green tufts of grass and runted trees and the air was fresh and warm.

She twisted in the seat to look behind them, but the narrow road was empty as far as the eye could see. "Where are we?" she asked as she turned to Quint.

The morning light touched his face, exposing lines etched deeply at his mouth and the shadow of a new beard at his jaw. He wasn't looking at her, yet the sight of him and his closeness hit her hard.

"We're about ready to drop down into Texas, then we've got a hundred miles to the New Mexico border. According to the signs I've been passing for the past half hour, gas and telephones should be just ahead over that hill. They'd better be there, because we're almost running on fumes."

She looked away and down the road. A sandwich sign propped on the side of the road announced Gas and Cold Drinks Ahead ½ Mile, but the only thing she could see was the empty road. Then they crested the hill and she spotted a clearing. In the middle was a flat-roofed building that looked like a store with powdery adobe walls. To one side, an old mobile home painted a lurid pink was propped up on wooden blocks.

A huge sign on the roof of the store was faded, but readable: Bill's Place—Cold Beer and Good Food. Three gas pumps shaded by a metal awning stood between the buildings and the road, and a banner strung from the top of the awning to the roof of the building swung in the gentle breeze. It read See the World's Finest Rattlesnake Exhibit.

"The signs didn't lie," Quint said as he drove off the road and headed to the gas pumps. Dust rose behind the black car, billowing into the warm air as he eased to a stop by the nearest pump. The door to the mobile home opened and a thin, elderly man in oil-stained overalls stepped out. He shaded his eyes with one hand, looked out at the car, then ambled down the wooden steps and across to the pumps.

"Help ya, mister?" he asked.

"Fill it with super," Quint said. Then, "Have you got any public phones?"

"Sure do. Right back there," he said and motioned to the right of the adobe store. "Rest room's back there, too, right by the rattlesnake cages."

Quint looked at Annie. "Make your call, and I'll get us some food and drinks."

"I'll be right back," she said and got out.

As she crossed the dusty parking lot, the old man called out to her, "Don't forget to see the snakes, Miss, it's free!"

She waved to him, then kept going around the side of the store and spotted a pay phone on the wall right across from the exhibit. There were several wood and wire raised cages that formed a semicircle and she didn't have to go any closer to see a snake coiled in each one.

Keeping as much distance between herself and the cages as she could, she went to the pay phone and put in the call to Jeannie. Thankfully, the line wasn't busy and Jeannie answered on the second ring. "Hello?"

"Jeannie?"

"Annie, it's you."

"Yes," she sighed. "It's me."

"Where are you?"

She looked around. "Heading toward New Mexico, about a hundred miles from the border."

"I was worried when we talked before, with your car dying on you and you hitching a ride with some trucker. I know you're desperate, but we could have come for you."

"I didn't have that much time. And things are all right now." She pressed her forehead against the cool metal of the phone case as she simplified her explanation for Jeannie. "I met someone who's giving me a ride."

"Who?"

"His name's Quint and he's going to California."

"Annie, you're crazy to be hitchhiking. God knows who you'll tangle with."

"I'm not hitchhiking. I met him and he offered to take me west. Believe me, I'm safe with him." That was so true. She felt more safe with Quint than with anyone she'd ever known. "He used to be a bodyguard. I mean, he's . . . he's . . ."

"Built like a gorilla, probably," Jeannie muttered. "How far is he taking you?"

"As far as I can get him to." She changed subjects quickly. "I don't have much time, but I wanted to talk to Sammi."

"Oh, sweetie, she's still asleep. But don't worry, she's being an angel."

Tears pricked the back of her eyes and she bit her lip hard to keep them under control. She needed to hear her daughter's voice, to have some connection. "Thanks for doing this for me," she whispered.

"Hey, are you sure you're all right?"

Besides having the police after her, she was just fine. "I'll survive."

"What about Trevor? Do you know what happened after you left him lying there?"

"He's fine, apparently. He's filed assault charges against me."

"You're kidding?"

"No, he's got the cops looking for me. And I'm sure he's going to be in Taos looking for me. We're going to have to figure out where to meet when I get there."

"I'll talk to Charlie and we'll settle on a place. When you get closer, call and we'll make arrangements."

"I will. Just take care of Sammi and . . . and tell her I love her."

"She knows that, sweetie. Just hurry up and get here. She needs you."

"I need her, too," she said, her voice breaking. She bit her lip hard. "I'll call when I'm an hour away."

She put the receiver back in the cradle, then turned and stared at the rattlesnakes in their cages. "Damn it all," she muttered and kicked at the rocky ground. Her sandal caught a pebble and sent it ricochetting over the dust to strike the leg of the nearest cage.

The snake immediately raised its head, the rattles on its tail vibrating menacingly. Annie turned away and hurried back around the building to the car. Quint was nowhere in sight, neither was the old man, so Annie got in and settled against the warm leather.

She looked up at the sign for the rattlesnake exhibit and thought that any rattlesnake was better than Trevor. The snake at least gave warning before it struck. Trevor just went in for the kill. First, he'd walked out on her when she got pregnant; then he thought he could use Sammi to get his inheritance. Now he was going to take Sammi away from her and have her jailed.

There was no way she was going to let that happen. No way. She slapped her hand flat on the console and felt something brush her bare leg. When she sat forward and looked down at her feet, she saw the envelope she'd put between the seat and the console lying on the carpet by her purse.

With a sigh, she reached for it and would have put it back in place but the printed return address caught her attention. Department of Corrections for the Commonwealth of Massachusetts. In the center was a typed name, Quinton James Gallagher, and a long number after it. She stared at it until her eyes ached from the glare of the sunlight on the bright white paper.

And she'd been worrying about being truthful with Quint! No wonder he didn't want to get involved with her and problems with the law. Her hand began to shake and she quickly turned the envelope over. Her breathing was suspended as she tucked her forefinger under the partially sealed flap and tugged at it. The glue gave way easily and the flap lifted to expose several sheets of folded paper.

She glanced nervously over her shoulder, but no one was there. She looked back at the open envelope, closed her eyes for just a moment, then tugged the folded papers out. As she scanned the packet, her throat tightened. She didn't know what the conviction numbers meant, but she knew what felony meant and what arrest and release dates were.

She pushed the papers back in the envelope and closed the flap. She'd told Jeannie she felt safe with Quint. But he had been in prison, and it looked as if he just got out days ago. She had no idea what he did, but a felony was serious business. A felony was robbery—or murder.

She couldn't begin to see Quint as threatening, but it was there in black and white. And she didn't know if she should get out of this car and run, or sit here and wait for him to explain. Or put back the envelope and pretend she never saw it.

She jumped when Quint called out, "Thanks for everything."

She turned and saw him coming out of the store, the strong morning light etching him with a clarity that was painful. He'd been her salvation, but at what cost? She'd heard about men who were charming and sweet, then turned out to be serial killers.

Charming and sweet? Quint had never tried to be either. But he'd been there when she needed him and touched her emotionally and physically in a way no other man ever had. She'd made mistakes, trusting people she never should have trusted, but something deep inside her kept her from getting out of the car and running.

As Quint came around the car, she watched him. He wasn't any different. And her response to him hadn't changed. She was glad to see him getting into the car and closing the door. And when he held a small grocery bag out to her, she laid the envelope on her lap and took the bag.

"I hope you like ham sandwiches and Coke," he said.

"That sounds fine," she murmured as she rested the bag on top of the envelope on her lap.

Quint looked at her for a long moment, his eyes narrowed in the brightness of the day, then he turned and started the car. He drove back out onto the highway, eased the car up to cruising speed, then said, "I could use a cold drink."

She took a cold can of soda out of the bag for Quint, handed it to him, then took out one for herself. All she had to do was ask, Why were you in prison? It was simple, but she was having trouble saying the words.

"Well, are you going to tell me what's wrong?" Quint asked after he took a drink.

"Excuse me?"

"Your phone call must have been bad news. You look like you got a real jolt."

Quickly she popped the tab on her can of soda and took a drink. She let the cool liquid slip down her throat, then she cradled the can in her hands. "I guess you could say that."

Quint knew something was wrong. He'd known it when he came back to the car and took one look at Annie. Her skin was tinged with paleness, and he could feel the tension in her. Heaven knew, he'd been around her enough in times of stress to recognize the symptoms, and he knew that something was very wrong now.

"Want to talk about it?" he asked.

She was silent for such a long time that he finally looked at her. She was staring at the can of soda as she pressed it against the inside of her left wrist. He quickly focused on the road, not the delicate bones of her wrist or the tanned expanse of leg exposed by the beige shorts. "Annie?"

"What?"

"Tell me what happened," he said as he pushed his half-full can into the space between the door and his seat. The hairs at the nape of his neck were tingling, a feeling he knew too well when something was wrong, and it was a feeling he hated. "Come on, after everything we've been through, don't do this to me."

"Do what to you?"

"Hold out on me. If I'm putting my butt on the line, I deserve the truth. What happened? Did Trevor get to your friend? Are the cops waiting for you in Taos? What?''

He heard the rustle of paper, and when he glanced at her, he saw her putting the grocery bag on the floor by her feet, then she sat back. Without a word, she held out a white envelope to him, and he didn't have to take it to know it held his parole papers.

Chapter Nine

"I deserve the truth, too," Annie said.

Quint snatched the envelope from her hand. He'd forgotten about it and seeing her with it made him realize how ugly his past had really been. He pushed the envelope under his seat, but didn't look at Annie again. He stared straight ahead, and he hated the way his breathing became tight. "You opened it," he said, not a question, but a statement of what he already knew. "I'm surprised."

"It was here and the flap wasn't stuck very well."

"Oh, not about you opening it. I sure as hell would have opened it if I'd been in your position. I'm surprised that you didn't jump out and run for your life."

"I thought about it," she said.

"Then you should have. I told you way back you could have been getting in the car with a psycho."

"I thought you were trying to scare me."

"I was," he said, his eyes burning and the images down the road beginning to blur. "And trying to get you to stay at your car and wait for help. But you insisted on coming with me."

"Why were you in . . . that place?"

"Prison, it was prison. A place where a person's not a person and the only respect you get is from other cons you beat up before they can go for you. A place where humanity is lost and you start living on the level of an animal. I was locked up for two years."

"Why?"

He didn't see any reason to sugarcoat it in any way. "I beat a man up. And I didn't just knock a drunk over, either. I would have probably killed him if I hadn't been stopped."

"Why would you—"

"He was raping a woman." The blunt words hung in the warm air.

"You found a man raping a woman?"

"Yeah." He laughed, a humorless, bitter sound. "I've come to realize that I really do have a built-in stupidity response. I see someone in trouble and I end up getting involved. Sort of the way I have with you."

"Why would you be arrested if that man was raping the woman?"

"The man bought the woman off, and she said it was consensual, that I overreacted and..." He took a deep breath. "Let's just leave it that no one believed me and I ended up cutting a deal. My attorney, the diligent Mr. Gray, got them to reduce attempted murder charges to aggravated assault. He felt good that he got me off easy, that I only lost two years of my life for doing a good deed. Go figure."

He didn't know what he expected when he finished talking, but it wasn't Annie to ask, "If it was happening again, what would you do?"

He saw a turn out ahead and pulled the car off the road onto crushed gravel. When he stopped, he took a steadying breath, then turned to Annie. "Would you knock Raines down if you had it to do again?"

"Yes, I probably would." Her green eyes were narrowed, but there wasn't the look of disgust or fear he expected to find there. She shook her head. "And so would you."

"How do you know that?"

"I know."

"Lady, you hardly know me."

"I've seen enough to know that you'd do the same thing. She was being raped, and you stepped in. You'd do it again." She shrugged, a fluttery movement of her slender shoulders. "Quint, look what you've done for me."

"I tried to dump you out on the road," he pointed out.

"You didn't."

"I was going to drag you out of this car bodily."

"You came back for me at the bus station. You didn't have to. You were in the clear, and you came back. I don't know much about being on parole, but I'm sure they wouldn't have just smiled and patted you on the head for helping me to get out of there."

He studied her face, and he hoped against hope that she didn't have some gift to look into his soul. He wasn't at all sure what she'd find there. But he knew that she was the first person to ever make him feel as if he had one. And that made him more uneasy than having the cops coming after him. "Lady, don't make me a hero," he said gruffly.

"I'm just thankful, that's all."

"What about now?"

"Excuse me?"

"Do you want me to let you out here, or do you feel safe being in this car with me a while longer?"

She fingered the can of soda she was holding but never looked away from him. Her mouth looked tight, and she spoke in a low voice. "I think I need to get away from you as soon as I possibly can."

His chest tightened. He'd wanted it to be over, to snatch back his life before he'd found that Annie was working her way into it. But he hated her words as she uttered them. "Sure, I understand," he said, even if he didn't understand the pain the words were causing him.

"No, you don't."

"A felon's not the best traveling partner."

"That's not it at all. I mean, the cops are after me. After everything you've done for me, I just can't let you get in any deeper. I had no idea what you were risking." Her smile was faint and unsteady. "I know you've got a built-in stupidity response, but I can stop this. I'm not going to let you get in trouble for me, so I'm going to get clear of you as soon as I can."

It had been so long since anyone worried about him, that Quint didn't know exactly how to react. "I can take care of myself," he muttered.

"I saw how you can take care of things at the diner. But I can't let you—"

He looked right at her. "Annie, let's get one thing straight right now. No one tells me what I can or can't do. Right now, I'm heading west, and you're heading west. I'll drive you as long as it's viable."

"But—"

"No, that's it. My car. My rules."

She bit her lip, but kept quiet.

"All right. Let's get going," he said, and it took him until he was back on the highway building speed before he realized that he'd just reversed roles with Annie. Now he was talking her into staying with him, instead of she trying to talk him into staying with her.

The whole world had gone crazy and he was at the front of the line. He didn't understand it, and he didn't try to. For now, he'd just accept the fact that Annie was still with him, and that having her there pushed back a loneliness he hadn't even known had invaded him until he met her.

As he built up more speed, he checked in the rearview mirror and a painful burst of adrenaline surged through him. Back maybe a quarter of a mile or so, he saw a single car...a state trooper's car. And any hope that it wasn't after them died when the lights switched on at the same time the siren's wail cut through the air.

Quint flashed a look at Annie, and she was twisting in the seat to look behind them. "Oh, no," she gasped, then her eyes met Quint's.

The adrenaline rush from fear right then didn't compare to the rush of protectiveness he felt for this woman. Commitment had never been in his vocabulary, but in a single heartbeat, he knew he was in this for the long haul. As the state trooper's car began to gain on them, Quint called to Annie, "Hold on," and pressed the gas pedal.

When Annie heard the siren, then turned and saw the flashing lights of the squad car coming after them, she'd thought it was all over. Until she looked at Quint. She heard him tell her to hold on and felt the car surge forward as he pressed the accelerator to the floor.

Tires squealed on the hot asphalt, and Annie felt herself pushed back into the seat by the force of the acceleration. Insanity had gone into madness, and she knew she should tell him to stop, to get out of this before he was in any deeper than he was already. But one look at the man and she kept quiet. A muscle worked at his jaw and his hands gripped the steering wheel in a death grip. He wasn't going to give up, and now she knew the fear behind his determination.

He was putting himself on the line, and she accepted his actions as a gift, the same way she was coming to accept the way she felt about the man himself. That last thought shocked her, and she looked at Quint again. Nothing seemed to matter, not the way they met, nor the way he tried to get rid of her, or his confession just moments ago. He'd burst into her life less than twenty-four hours ago, yet she knew that if she let herself feel anything beyond fear of the Raineses and impatience to get to Sammi, she could fall in love with this stranger.

She closed her eyes against this admission, as if the simple act could stop the thoughts as easily as the sight of the man could make her heart race. It was stupidity, her own built-in stupidity response. Yet she couldn't get past that totally foreign sensation of belonging and feeling safe when he held her.

Her thought process was shattered when she felt the car skid to the left and heard Quint mutter a harsh curse. She opened her eyes as the car skidded sideways on the highway, then caught traction and swung to the left onto a side road strewn with potholes. The acrid odor of burning rubber and the wail of sirens seemed to be everywhere, the makings of a chase in a grade B movie. But one look behind them, and Annie knew this wasn't make-believe.

The police were real. Their threat was real, and so was this man close to her, no matter what his past had been. It took her a moment to realize that the police car was falling farther back, shrinking into a speck in the distance. And she lost sight of it completely when they took a corner so hard it threw her against the door. The car fishtailed, then straightened out and surged forward through a land of low hills and dried brush.

She gripped the door handle so tightly her hand ached, and she turned to Quint. "This is crazy," she called out to him, partly acknowledging the insanity of her own scrambled feelings and partly acknowledging the insanity of him trying to outrun a police car.

He cast her a quick look, his dark eyes narrowed in the brightness of the day. "Do we have another option?" he yelled over the rush of hot air and wailing sirens.

She didn't have an option when it came to her feelings, but he certainly had an option to get out while the getting was good. "You can stop."

She didn't realize how afraid she was that he might do that very thing, until he shook his head and built more speed on the potted road.

"I think we're both in this too deep to do that," he said, his words almost snatched away before they could be heard in the rushing air. "I'm not going back to prison, and you sure as hell don't need to ever know what it is to be locked up like an animal."

"Quint, this is my problem, not yours," she yelled at him, knowing the truth of the words as they formed. He was a stranger, a man pulled into this by fate and circumstances. A man who could end up back in prison for doing a good deed. "I can't let you—"

He cut off her words with, "No one lets me do anything," then he looked back at the road and concentrated on his driving.

She knew that Quint did what he wanted, when he wanted and how he wanted to do it. She just didn't know why he was doing this. And any answers she thought of, she pushed away. It was too dangerous to let her imagination fashion reasons that she wanted to hear. He was saving his own skin. Period.

She looked away as Quint grimly negotiated pothole after pothole, and the powerful car didn't hesitate as the road began to climb. Higher hills appeared on both sides along with larger trees and more ground cover. They crested a hill, then went down into a lower area where the road forked right and left. The right branch headed down farther into a wide valley area, and the fork to the left cut into trees on a road that went up into the hills.

When they got close, Quint down-shifted, swung the car to the left and for a second, Annie thought the car was on two wheels. It shuddered, then Quint had it under control. He pressed the gas, and they headed upward into a changing land with trees crowding the road. When Quint began to slow, Annie could see him scanning the area, then he jammed on his brakes and turned onto broken asphalt that cut between thick trees.

The road went no more then a hundred yards before it came to an abrupt end in a washed-out area that looked as if it had been formed by a flash flood that had come out of the higher hills. A river of hard, swirl-cut sand washed through a basin strewn with rocks and tree parts. Then it disappeared to the south into more trees and rocks.

Quint eased the car onto the baked sand, then went to the right, over to spreading trees and stopped under the low branches of a red-barked tree. He turned off the engine and twisted in the seat to look back at the opening they'd just come through. Annie could tell he was holding his breath the same way she was as the sound of the sirens came closer and closer.

Then gradually, the sound began to fade off into the distance, and after what seemed an eternity, the sound was gone completely. The only noise was the low hum of insects in the hot air.

Quint sank back in the seat, exhaling roughly as he ran a hand over his face. But he looked far from relieved. "Damn, I never saw them coming until they were there."

"Neither did I," Annie said. She'd been too tied up in what Quint had been telling her, and trying to talk him into letting her leave him for his own good.

"The last thing I expected to be doing right about now was out-running the cops."

She sat back in the seat. "I should have made you let me out back there. Then even if they stopped you, it wouldn't matter."

"You're forgetting your truck driver. I'm sure he's not about to forget his throbbing kneecap."

"God, I'm so sorry," she breathed.

"Would you stop that."

She looked at him. "What?"

"Feeling sorry for me."

"It's not that. I just don't want you going back to... to that place."

"Prison, Annie, prison."

"And you just got out?"

He leaned his head back on the seat and stared at the clear sky through the branches of the tree. Tension etched his face with deep brackets at his mouth and fanned lines at his narrowed eyes. "A few days ago."

She swallowed hard, the idea of this man being locked up almost painful for her to think about. "Did you get your scar there?"

"No, I got that just before they locked me up. I'm lucky I didn't lose my eye."

"I'm sorry."

"Stop that, I—"

"I know, I know."

"That's the past." His expression when he turned to look at her was still etched with tension that made her nerves tingle. "Now it's California or bust."

If Annie could have turned back time, she would have. She would have never drawn Quint into this mess. She would have let him go to California and start his new life. The only problem with that was she would never have met him. And she was selfish enough to admit that she wouldn't have wanted to change that for a minute.

She looked away from Quint and opened the glove compartment. She pulled out the map, opened it and held it out to Quint. "Where are we on this?"

He took it from her and studied it, then pointed to a spot in northernmost Texas right by the New Mexico border. "Right about here," he said.

She looked at it. "I didn't even know we'd gotten into Texas."

"We're almost out of it. The New Mexico border's right up ahead."

She couldn't see any towns of any size between where they were and well toward Taos. "What town's the closest to us?"

He looked at it, then handed it back to her. "Taos."

"No, I mean, a place where I can rent a car or—"

"We can't take the chance of stopping in another Jarvis. This car stands out like a sore thumb in this country, and..." He looked at her so intently that she could feel her breathing start to constrict. "You don't just blend in either."

He cut off any response from her by starting the car again, and circled it on the packed sand to head back to the road. "We need to get out of this place. If the cops have an ounce of intelligence, they'll be back-tracking any time now."

Quint eased back through the opening in the trees, cautiously looked out onto the road and turned off the motor again. He listened for a long time, then started the car and moved out onto the road to turn right and head upward again.

"Quint?"

He cast Annie a slanted glance. "What?"

"You should have stopped back there."

Quint regripped the steering wheel. The rush of adrenaline was tapering off, and the spontaneous decision he'd made to get the hell out of there when he spotted the trooper's car was starting to look like a form of slow suicide to him.

Until he remembered the look on Annie's face. Then it made perfect sense. "They would have dragged me in on assault charges, parole violation, and probably something akin to accessory after the fact.''

''That's crazy. I forced you to take me with you. That's hardly being an accessory, and they couldn't press assault charges, not when they understood what that trucker was trying to do.''

''Just what was he trying to do when I broke in on the two of you?''

''Well, he wasn't proposing marriage,'' she muttered. ''My point is, I could tell them everything, and—''

''You ran. You didn't even see the fight.''

''The truth is the truth. It's that simple.''

The truth hadn't ever helped him very much before, and right now, it wasn't going to help anyone. Nothing was simple, not anymore than it had been since he'd first set eyes on this woman. ''The truth is I'm a convicted felon. That's sort of like being guilty until proven innocent. A parole violation can mean a straight year with no good time. I don't think talking would have cut it.''

''We could have tried.''

''Let me put this as simply as possible. I was saving my own skin back there, and you got pulled along in the process.''

''When we get to the next town, I don't care how big it is, you let me out.''

''Annie, that's suicide.''

''If you don't let me out, that's kidnapping.''

His burst of laughter startled her, and when she looked at Quint, she saw a man filled with humor, a man who looked younger and startlingly attractive. ''This is starting to sound like that story where two bumbling crooks kidnap a kid, and by the time they're done, they're paying his family to take him back."

"Well, there's no one willing to pay for my return," she said, then knew how wrong she was. And the laughter died.

"Even with his money, he's not going to win," Quint said unexpectedly.

"How can you be so sure?"

Quint exhaled, then said, "Because I've seen you in action, lady."

"I'm not going to go quietly, that's for sure," she said.

"Good. Now we need to figure out a way for us to lay low for a while."

She watched the way the sunlight being broken by the outspread branches of the trees that lined the road flashed across his face. "What?"

"Translated from the common prison vernacular, to lay low means to find a place where we can get out of sight, stop and wait until we've got a chance to get past the law."

"You mean we're just going to stop?"

"That's the plan."

"No, it's not," she said, sitting up straight in the seat. "We can't stop, not now. We have to keep going. We're almost in New Mexico. Then it's only—"

"Didn't you hear me? The cops are going to be coming after us any minute now. I don't know about you, but I'm not up for another chase. Besides, we were damned lucky last time. We could have just as easily been cut off and caught."

"Quint, just get to the next town."

"And they'll be waiting. We'll walk into their open arms and it's all over."

Now she wasn't only worrying about Sammi, but about Quint, too. And she felt as if she had the weight of the world on her shoulders. She didn't want either one to be hurt. "Then drop me on the outskirts, and—"

He hit the brakes and brought the car to a skidding stop near the shoulder of the road. Then he turned his dark gaze on her. "Listen to me, and understand what I'm saying. *We* need to hide." He said each word slowly, carefully enunciating each syllable as if she were a two-year-old getting a lesson and emphasizing the we. "*We* can not be seen on the road or in town, or I go back to prison and you go to jail or back to good old Trevor. And I haven't come this far to let any of the above happen."

She sank back in her seat, but when she started to tell him she would take her chances on her own, he cut her off.

"And don't think of walking from here. The next town is miles away, and they'll get you before you work up a sweat."

"Okay, it's your car, your rules. You've got the upper hand, but we can't stop for long."

"Until it's dark," he said.

"Just until six o'clock."

"No, nine. It should be completely dark by then."

She hesitated. "Seven, and it should be getting dusky by then."

He shook his head. "No, the earliest we can show ourselves is eight."

She bit her lip, but ended up agreeing. "Eight."

"Good," he affirmed.

"Now," she said as she brushed at her hair, "let's find some place to lay low, as you say."

"Exactly," he returned and pulled back out on the road. As they drove in silence, Quint realized he'd just made a deal with Annie. She was in his car, using his gas, putting his tail on the line and she was actually bargaining with him.

"If we're going to stop," she finally said, "I hardly think we're going to find a motel or hotel around here."

"Who mentioned a motel or hotel?"

"I'm not sleeping in this car again," she declared quickly.

He wasn't at all sure he could do any resting in this car with her close by, not when he remembered all too well the last time he let himself fall asleep near her.

"We'll find something," he replied when he spotted a side road.

He slowed, then turned onto it. Trees pressed in on either side and low brush choked the ground. It didn't look as if anyone had been on the road for a long time. Weeds shot up through cracks in the blacktop, and tree branches were so low that any car sitting higher than the Corvette, would have been whipped by them.

"What's up here?" Annie asked.

"Nothing but isolation, I hope."

He followed the road, rounded a corner, and came upon a rusted chain strung across the road from heavy iron posts partially covered by wild brush. A metal sign with rust holes in it was wired to the chain: No Trespassing.

"I guess that's it," Annie said.

"We'll see," Quint replied as he got out and crossed to the chain. He checked where it was attached to the posts. Wire held it in place on the one side, and the wire was almost rusted through. Gripping the chain with both hands, he jerked back on it as hard as he could and the wire popped.

He dropped the chain, went back to the car and got in. When he drove forward over the chain, Annie said quickly, "You can't do that. This is someone's property."

He cast her a quick look, never used to the way his whole being seemed to come alive just at the sight of her. "I hardly think after evading arrest, we have to worry about a little thing like trespassing."

"But you can't just—"

He cut off her words by stopping the car and getting out to head back to the opening. He pulled the chain back across the road, used the rusted wire to hold it in place, then he went back to the car.

"Don't look a gift horse in the mouth," he muttered as he got back in.

"How about, necessity is the mother of invention?" she asked.

He looked at her, the sunlight dappling through the boughs overhead, touching her face with a delicate beauty that all but took his breath away. Humor was the last thing on his mind right then, but he managed, "Crime, like virtue, has its degrees." He put the car in gear. "And this is a very small crime and a necessary one. Trust me, I know."

Chapter Ten

Quint drove forward, up the winding road until it crested and leveled out into a meadowlike clearing. The road ended right in front of a small, dilapidated cabin in the middle of dry grass and wildflowers.

He went as far as he could, then stopped the car, and pressed the horn. The harsh blare echoed around the clearing, then he hit the horn again. No one appeared at the door or from behind the cabin. "It looks deserted. I think we just found a place to stop for a while."

When he would have gotten out, Annie grabbed him by the arm, and the contact made him freeze. Even as he turned to face her, her connection with him was almost searing. "What now?"

"You aren't going to break into that house, are you?"

"I'm going to visit the owner," he muttered and pulled free of her touch so he could think clearly.

She let him go, but she didn't back down a bit. "Someone might not mind you coming onto his land, but you really can't take over his home."

"Watch me," he said and got out, needing distance to take a deep breath without the air being touched by the scent of Annie.

He heard her coming after him, but he didn't hesitate as he took the two steps to the sagging porch in one stride. He crossed, grabbed the latch and thankfully it gave way without much effort. Then the door swung back on creaking hinges and he stepped into the house.

As his eyes adjusted to the dimness, he could make out a single room with a peaked ceiling, plank flooring and two small windows at the back covered by pieces of red-and-white checked material. The space was no more than twenty-by-twenty feet, and sparsely furnished with an iron-frame bed, stripped, the linen piled on the mattress by the footboard and a small table with a single chair. There was a potbellied stove, a huge cabinet on the back wall next to a free-standing sink and some threadbare throw rugs on the floor.

It made him feel closed in, almost trapped, but it would do for Annie. He could stay in the car and rest as long as she wasn't too close to him. He needed to move and he crossed to a draped doorway on the right to draw back the gray material. He saw an old-fashioned pull toilet, a shower stall framed by metal and glass, and a sink with rust staining the porcelain.

As he let the material fall back in place, he turned and found Annie on the porch in the open doorway. "The maid service looks pretty deplorable, but it's got indoor plumbing. Nothing fancy, but it's all there."

"We can't just come in here like this," she said, not moving.

He spread his arms at his sides. "Get over it, Annie. We're in here, and we're here until eight o'clock.

You can stay in the car or stay in here. It's your choice."

He couldn't keep looking at her with the sun at her back, her hair rich copper and her long legs bared in the shorts. So he turned and opened the cabinet and found a sparse selection of canned goods, a few dishes and on the bottom shelf, some extra linen. Everything had the odor of being closed for a very long time, a staleness that needed fresh air and sunshine to banish it.

"If it makes you feel any better, we'll leave some money to cover our time here," he said as he closed the cupboard door.

He heard her move behind him, and when he turned around, she was a few feet from him. The soft light in the cabin blurred her features slightly, but that didn't stop his instant response to her. Or the small space shrinking even more until he could hear each breath she took.

"I guess, if you leave money, it wouldn't be like just using the place," she murmured.

"Good." He moved past her without inhaling and went to the door. "While I get some things out of the car, why don't you check and see if the plumbing works."

Annie moved to let him pass, feeling the oddest sense of contact with him when none was made. She seemed to just inhale and catch at him, then he was gone and heading out the door and down the steps to the car. She turned back to the room, then crossed to the sink and turned on the spigot. Water ran slowly out of it into the chipped sink, cold and clean.

"You've got the bed," Quint said from behind her, startling her.

She fumbled to turn off the spigot then turned. He was by the foot of the bed, and he'd stripped off his T-shirt and discarded it on top of his duffel bag that was sitting on the floor beside her suitcase at his feet. The sight of him bare-chested made her mouth go dry and she felt like a teenager in the throes of a stupid crush. She had to force herself not to look at his bare chest and the suggestive sprinkling of hair that formed an arrow downward.

And the idea of a bed right now was unsettling. "No," she said as she stared at a spot near his right shoulder. "You can have it. You're the one driving."

"I'm not used to anything that resembles comfort. And I hate being closed in." He smiled, a rueful expression, almost apologetic. "Tight places just aren't that appealing to me right now. Take the bed, and I'll stretch out on the porch with a couple of the blankets or in the car. Trust me, I won't miss a mattress."

His words were said with a degree of lightness, but she could hear an underlying uneasiness in them. "Okay, I'll take the bed."

"Good, a woman who's agreeable. Now, how's the water situation?"

"It's on, but it's cold."

"There's a generator in a shed up the side, but I don't think there's any fuel to start it up. If we take showers, they'll have to be cold."

"Any sort of shower sounds good to me," Annie murmured.

"Me, too," he said as he crossed to the curtained doorway. "Heads or tails?"

"Excuse me?"

"We'll flip for first use of the plumbing facilities," he said as he pushed his hand into the pocket of his jeans and pulled out a quarter.

"Heads," she murmured, and Quint tossed the quarter in the air, then caught it between the back of his forearm and his palm.

"Heads," he said as he looked under his hand, then back at Annie. "Luck's with you."

"I hope so," she whispered and went to pick up her suitcase by the bed.

When she approached the curtained door, Quint stopped her by saying her name. "Annie?"

She stopped, but didn't look up at him. "What?"

"I'm taking you to Taos. I'm not dropping you in some hick town. And that isn't open to discussion."

She felt the sting of tears behind her eyes, and she knew she couldn't look at Quint right then. She didn't know what to say, so she nodded, then ducked past the gray curtain into the bathroom.

She quickly put down her suitcase and turned on the water in the small stall. Without giving herself time to think, she stripped off her clothes, then eased in under the cold water. At first she began to shake from the cold, then as the water ran over her, tears came. She had never been one to cry. She just coped and went on, but the tears came the way they had in the rest room at the bus station, without rhyme or reason. And they didn't stop until she was spent and so cold her teeth were chattering.

WHEN QUINT CAME OUT of the bathroom after his shower an hour later, Annie was nowhere in sight. His last glimpse of her had been when she'd stepped out of the cabin after her shower, with her hair wet and lying close to her head. She'd dressed in white shorts and a navy tank top, and her feet bare when she dropped down on the top step of the porch.

He walked across the empty cabin, then spotted her through the open door, still sitting where he'd left her. Her hair was drying and curling crazily around her shoulders, turned to fire in the rays of the sun that broke through the trees. She sat very still, her arms wrapped around her bent legs and her chin rested on her knees.

He'd meant it when he'd told her he'd get her to Taos, even though she didn't say a thing when he made the statement. And he hadn't been prepared for how it made him feel when he heard her crying when the shower hadn't been able to hide the sounds.

He'd heard people cry, grown men sobbing, but nothing had touched him as deeply as when he heard her cry. First in the men's room when he'd held her and hadn't understood. Then the sounds of sobs coming from the shower. She was scared, and he knew that if Trevor Raines was here right now, he'd be hard put to not kill the guy.

He raked his fingers through his damp hair, skimming it back from his face, then he padded barefoot to the door. He'd always hated jerks, no matter where he met them, but this was different. He wanted to keep Annie safe, to keep hurt and pain away from her, and that was everything that Trevor seemed to mean to her.

When he saw her shoulders trembling, he almost turned and walked back into the cabin. But before he could silently escape, she spoke to him.

"It's so peaceful here, isn't it?" she said softly.

He felt anything but peaceful right now. "It's quiet, that's for sure," he said from the doorway.

"No, it's more than that. It gives you the feeling that nothing can intrude, that the ugliness in life just doesn't exist." Her rueful chuckle was very soft. "What a lie. Even a place like this won't make Trevor disappear in a puff of smoke."

He suddenly wished he had it in his power to give her a place like that, a world where there was no ugliness or pain. The irony of that thought wasn't lost on him. An ex-con on parole couldn't give anyone peace, including himself. "No, it's still part of the world," he said.

"It wasn't the money with Trevor," she said abruptly. "I want you to know that. It never was the money. It was the things he had that I never had, family, roots, a place that was really home." She shifted and hugged her arms around herself. "I'm so scared."

"About Trevor?" he asked without moving.

"Yes, him, but other things even more."

"What other things?"

She inhaled, and he saw the unsteadiness in her shoulders. "I owe you an explanation."

"You've told me everything I need to know."

"No, I haven't."

He stood very still, and he knew exactly what she was going to say. And he wasn't sure he wanted to hear it. He'd pushed the name she'd screamed in her nightmare out of his mind. But now he knew it was coming back to haunt him. "What didn't you tell me?"

"There's someone."

His being tightened. "Sam?"

That brought a startled reaction from her. She twisted to look at him over her shoulder. "What did you say?"

He had to work at not clenching his jaw. "Sam, your friend in Taos."

"Oh, boy, have you got it all wrong," she said and turned away with a shaky laugh.

His nerves were stretched to the breaking point, and there was no way he found this amusing. He crossed the small porch and strode past Annie to go down the stairs. Then he turned and he was almost at eye level with her as she sat on the top step. "This isn't funny."

She shook her head, then stretched out her legs and pressed her hands flat on the wooden floor of the porch at her sides. "No, it's not. But how did you know about Sammi?"

"When you had your nightmare in the car, you called out to him."

She closed her eyes and exhaled softly. "Oh, that's how."

"Annie, what is he to you?"

"I'd better start at the beginning."

"Just tell me the truth."

She sat forward and spread her slender hands on her thighs. "It's true that I was going to marry Trevor, that I heard him talking, that he got ugly when I confronted him, that I left him lying on the ground unconscious and ran. That I'm not going to go back, no matter what he tries. It's probably true that he's not going to give up, even when I get to Taos and disappear."

He could see the way her hold on her legs tightened with each word she said. "Because of your involvement with this Sam person?"

"Yes."

Quint didn't realize until right then how much he'd wanted anything but that answer. Stupidity seemed to be all he did well lately. "I see."

"No, you don't."

He looked at her, wishing she was ugly and as undesirable as a fence post. But she wasn't. The sun exposed the delicate beauty of her face, and the intensity in her eyes. "What don't I understand? You had someone else, thought you could go through with a wedding to Trevor so you could be part of the Raines family, then got cold feet. Isn't that about it?"

"No."

Bitterness burned his throat. "Then why don't you tell me what's going on with you and use plain English, Annie."

"Plain English." She hesitated, then said, "Sam is actually Samantha, usually called Sammi."

"What?"

"And Trevor's never going to give up, even if I get to Taos, because he wants our daughter."

The statement sent him reeling. "Sam . . . Sammi is your daughter?"

"Yes."

"Oh, God," he muttered, no boyfriend, but a child. He turned from Annie, trying to absorb what she'd just said. But as the truth settled into him, he realized something else, something ugly and frightening. He clenched his hands at his sides, then turned back to face her.

"Let me get this straight. You and Trevor have a child, and you tried to kill him because you've got her hidden someplace?"

"I didn't try to kill him, but I probably thought about it. But he was getting rough and ugly and I just got out."

Sir Galahad? A knight in shining armor? Despite two years in hell for charging in where he shouldn't have, he'd done it again. But this time he'd burst into a child custody battle that seemed to be going from ugly to dangerous. "Oh, man."

"Quint, let me explain."

"No, let me guess. Trevor's got every cop in this territory gunning for you, because you kidnapped his kid?"

She spread her hands palms up. "No, she's with my friends. She's safe and that's the way she's going to stay. Trevor only wants Sammi because she's the Raineses' only grandchild, and she gives him a handle on all that money."

"You've lost me."

"Trevor doesn't care about Sammi. When he found out I was pregnant, he never even contacted me. He never returned my letters. He wasn't there when she was born, or when she said her first word, or when she took her first step. He didn't even see her until two months ago."

She bit her lip hard. "He showed up at my doorstep in Taos professing his undying love for both of us. Telling me what a fool he'd been to let me go and to have missed so much of Sammi's life. And I bought into it."

Her voice was getting more and more unsteady, until she had to stop and take a breath before she could go on. And whatever anger Quint had been harboring was rapidly slipping away from him. "His parents found out about the baby and gave him an ultimatum. Get their grandchild and marry her mother, or get out.

"The Raineses are very big on bloodlines and family and protocol. So, I came to the ranch with Sammi, to this wonderful place with horses and wide open spaces and grandparents...and I let myself get caught up in it."

"How did the kid get to Taos?"

"My friend, Jeannie, and her husband, Charlie, were invited to a party the Raineses gave to introduce me to their friends last week, and I let Sammi go back with them until the wedding. I thought if I had some time alone with Trevor, that things might change. That I might be able to figure out what I was doing."

"Did you love him?" he asked, his voice tight in his own ears. But he had to know.

She never looked away from Quint. "No. I know that now. Oh, I wanted to. I wanted to make Sammi's life better than anything I could give her and I would have married him. Then I overheard Trevor in the barn telling his friend about his parents' pressure on him and that if I gave him any trouble about seeing other women, he'd convince his parents that I wasn't a good mother and have me thrown out."

She shrugged. "Then Trevor spotted me and you know the rest. The Raineses have all the advantages in the situation, so I wasn't going to stay around and settle this with them. On top of that, I knocked out their son. As much as they get angry at him, he's the world to them."

"So, you ran." Not a question, just a statement of fact.

"Yes, I ran. Now, I'm going to get Sammi and disappear. I've been on my own with Sammi from the start, and I can do it again."

He knew she could. But he also knew she shouldn't have to. "How old is she?"

"Twenty-two months."

He ran a hand roughly over his face. A child. Her child. "She's at your friend's home in Taos?"

She hesitated. "I don't think I should tell you exactly where she is, just in case—"

That touched a nerve and he strode back to her, barely keeping himself from grabbing her by her shoulders and shaking some sense into her. "What in the hell? Do you think I'd run into your ex-fiancé and spill my guts or work out a plea bargain with the authorities if they picked me up?"

Her eyes were wide, but she didn't back down. "No, but the less you know the less trouble you can get into."

"Lady, in case you didn't notice, I'm up to my hips in your trouble. Another couple of inches isn't going to drown me."

"I don't want you to—"

He went closer, any anger he'd had when she told him the last part of her story was gone. And something else had taken its place. "I've told you over and over again, don't worry about me."

He found himself reaching out and touching her chin with one finger. "You're doing this all for the kid, aren't you?"

"Yes." She shrugged. "And if anything ever happened to me, she wouldn't be alone. I thought . . . I let myself think that if I let the Raineses take us in,

Sammi would have it all. Security, a family, love, caring. And a real father. That was a joke."

"You made a mistake," he said softly, unnerved by the trembling in her jaw.

"Boy, did I ever. I mean, I knew I didn't love Trevor, but love didn't seem necessary. Other things would have made up for it. But I couldn't let him use Sammi like that. She's wonderful. She's so special, Quint, and she deserves so much more than I can give her."

"Hey, you're giving your child a lot more than most kids get."

She looked at him, her eyes overly bright, and he prayed that she wouldn't cry. "What?"

"You love her. Any kid would be fortunate to have someone love them like you love her." Any man would be more than fortunate to have this woman's love. And it stunned him that he was actually having twinges of what might have been jealousy for a little child he'd never even met. "You can't fake that, or buy that, or demand that," he said, his voice rough.

She closed her eyes for a long moment and he knew she was trying to gather her control. And he hated it. He'd seen it often enough, her trying to tamp down her fears and uncertainties, literally holding herself together. And he wanted to be there for her, to give her a place to cry and rage if she wanted to, a place where she was safe and happy.

God, this woman touched him on levels he couldn't begin to comprehend.

"Hey," he said softly and let himself gently cup her chin. "Quit beating yourself up, Annie. Sammi's a damn lucky kid."

Annie opened her eyes, the green deep and vibrant with unshed tears and when her tongue touched her pale lips, he knew that he was damn lucky himself to be here with her. Damn lucky she pulled him into her life and held on until he didn't want to let go.

He knew he didn't have any right to feel the way he was feeling. He wasn't what she needed or what she wanted, and he sure couldn't give her the things she deserved, but on a selfish level, he wanted her. Once, just once, he wanted to know her, to touch her, to explore her and to feel her against him.

And he did what he'd wanted to do for every second of every minute of every hour since he'd first met her. He lowered his head, touched his lips to hers, and the instant he caught the taste of her in his mouth and felt her softness against him, he was lost.

For a heartbeat Annie didn't move, then with a shuddering sigh, she seemed to collapse against him. Her arms went around his neck, and her lips opened in invitation. And the passion that had been there with each touch from the first, exploded into an aching need that threatened to consume Quint.

The place she'd spoken of, that place where no ugliness could intrude, was here and now. It was real, as real as the feeling of her tongue teasing his, the feeling of her breasts pressed to his chest. She held on to him, arching against him, and he ran his hand over her back, over tensed muscles, then he drew back.

Her eyes were heavy with desire, and her lips were swollen from the kisses. And he knew if he was going to stop this, it had to be now, no matter what the price for him. He framed her face with his hands and he looked into a face that he knew he could love. He trembled at that thought, then knew it wasn't a matter of "could" any more.

He loved Annie.

God help him, but she'd burst into his world and given him life. A life he'd never had before. And even when they were running from the cops or hiding, he was more alive now than he ever remembered being.

The words were there, the words to tell her how he felt, but they wouldn't come. They couldn't. He didn't have the right to love this woman.

When her hand lifted to brush his cheek, he froze. Then she touched his scar. The contact was as light as a feather, but it was so intense that he had to close his eyes to absorb the feelings. Then Annie moved. She kissed the damaged skin, and he felt as if her touch could heal his soul.

God, that's what he needed. He needed to be whole, to find the part of him he thought he'd lost forever, and she was here. He shuddered when her hands spread on his chest, and the contact seared him through the thin cotton of his T-shirt. He lost the ability and will to do anything more than feel and sense and absorb this woman's presence.

Chapter Eleven

With his eyes closed, Quint could feel everything more clearly, the way her fingers splayed over his chest, the way her thigh was pressed to his, the way her breath seemed to bathe him in gentle heat. Slowly, her hands worked their way under his shirt, and he realized how desperate he was for skin on skin contact. Softness, silky heat, comfort, losing himself, freeing himself from everyday life, from just existing.

He opened his eyes and looked into the emerald green of hers, seeing the echo of his own feelings deep in her gaze. Then he moved, in some way getting them both to their feet. With a rightness that staggered him, he drew her to him and they simply held on tight for what could have been an eternity or maybe just a heartbeat.

When she breathed his name and lifted her face to his, whatever control he'd been trying to maintain was gone. With a low groan, he captured her mouth as his hands stroked her back, then dropped to her hips. He cupped her bottom, then lifted her up to him. Her arms wound around his neck and her fingers tangled in his hair, then her legs wrapped tightly around his waist.

Quint twisted to the side and pressed Annie back against the rough wall, ravishing her with his tongue and willing her even closer with his hands. She put her head back, exposing the sweep of her throat to his kisses and he tasted the sweetness of her skin, then the soft cleavage where her shirt parted just above her breasts.

For a second he thought of stopping it all. He thought of telling her to run and keep running, that a man like him was as much a threat to her as Trevor ever could be. But he wasn't that noble. He wasn't even close. He felt her body against his, her legs surrounding him, and her touch on his back, and he knew that nobility was sadly lacking in him.

Passion that should have built gradually was there in full force for Annie, exploding in her with white hot fire. The touch of the man sent her reeling, and the knowledge that she could be making a mistake was lost under the avalanche of ecstasy that surrounded and threatened to drown her. She held on to Quint, tasting him, feeling his touch on her, then he was carrying her into the cabin.

She buried her face in his neck, and as they fell back onto the stripped bed together, she didn't let go of him. She kept her legs around his hips, and found herself under him, looking up into his midnight brown eyes. And the passion became all consuming. Awkwardly she tried to lift her tank top to take it off, but her fingers refused to cooperate. Then Quint was on his knees between her legs and he reached for the soft material. He tugged it up, over her head and slid it off her arms.

She hadn't put on a bra after her shower, and her breasts were naked. When she looked up at Quint, her nipples tightened, and she heard Quint groan, a low sound at the back of his throat. But he didn't move. He didn't touch her. He simply looked at her with a fiery hunger that took her breath away.

She reached for his hands, then drew them to her breasts, wanting his touch on her. And slowly his hands cupped her breasts and she arched toward him. Slowly his thumbs teased her nipples, and she moaned softly, shards of sensations shooting through her, down into her belly. Then Quint bent over her, his lips and tongue finding what his hands had just felt, and he drew her nipple into his mouth.

"Oh, yes," she whispered, and his hands moved lower, pushing aside the cotton of her shorts. And some way the shorts were gone, then her panties were slipped off her legs, and she lay naked under Quint.

Quint's hands moved over her, touching, feeling, teasing and building more fire with each caress. She crushed the cotton of his T-shirt in her hands, then tugged at it, needing to feel his skin against hers, his heat mingling with hers. For a brief moment, Quint moved back, and she opened her eyes to find him on his knees, tugging the T-shirt off to expose his bare chest.

She reached out, needing to feel him, but he moved even farther from her. She scrambled to her knees when he slipped off the bed and stood by the side. She reached out and touched the snap at the waist of his jeans, and she could feel his arousal under the denim. She looked up and saw him close his eyes and tip his head back as she slowly ran her hands up and down by the zipper. He trembled, then covered her hands with his to stop the motion.

With a shuddering breath he tugged at the snap, slid down the zipper, and stepped out of the jeans, leaving him in just his undershorts. The stark white against his skin was as sensual as anything Annie had ever seen, and to have the physical proof of his need for her only made things seem more right.

She touched the elastic waist of his shorts, then Quint helped her pull the cotton down until he was in front of her as naked as she was. For a brief moment she saw him fully and she reached out to him. Then he was back on the bed with her, his legs parting hers, and he braced himself with his hands flat on either side of her shoulders.

She looked up at him, his dark hair falling forward to partially shadow his face. She reached up to grip his shoulders and pulled him down to her.

She felt his strength testing her, and when she lifted her hips in invitation, he slid into her, filling her slowly and surely with shuddering intensity. She tried to lift her hips even higher, wanting him to be as deeply inside as was possible.

Then he began to move and she matched his rhythm, faster and faster, until there was nothing but shimmering ecstasy and love. When Annie dug her fingers into his shoulders, holding on in case she flew into a million pieces of joy, she felt Quint thrust harder and harder, forcing her higher and higher.

And when he climaxed, Annie met him, and she felt him take her with him to a place that she never knew existed before. A place where it was just him and her riding out wave after wave of pleasure and completion.

Annie stayed very still for a long time after she and Quint settled back in the bed. She was against his side, his arm around her, her head resting in the hollow of his shoulder, and his legs resting heavily over her thighs. She didn't move, afraid if she did that this would all evaporate and she'd find out she was dreaming.

She slowly inhaled, taking his scent, and she concentrated on the feeling of his body where it touched hers. His heart beat against her cheek, and the soft sounds of his breathing rippled through her. Oh, he was real. Very real, not a dream, and loving him was the easiest thing she'd ever done.

Love. She let the word sink into her being, and she knew how right it sounded. She loved this man with his dark eyes, his gentle touch and the ability to build a hunger in her that only he could satisfy. Even now, sated with the pleasures he'd given her, she could feel the stirring of need coming again. An ache formed deep inside her, sending a tingling message through her, and she spread her hand on his stomach.

She shifted to press her lips to his chest, and she felt him take a low, shuddering breath. When she eased back and lifted on one elbow, she found his dark eyes on her, and the stirring in her intensified.

She reached up and touched the scar that cut over his eye. "A bottle?"

"I didn't duck fast enough to miss getting clobbered with a half-full bottle of Dom Pérignon. Sort of a status symbol in prison. Others had scars from knives and metal and soda bottles, but not from a vintage champagne bottle."

Even though he was making light of it, her heart broke for what he'd been through. She remembered the moment he'd come to her, the intensity of his need and the gentleness of his touch. She trailed her finger over his skin, the freshly shaved jaw, then down his neck to the hollow where a pulse beat furiously. So she wasn't the only one who was feeling that need again.

"It must have been horrible in that place," she whispered. "I can't imagine what it would be like. And you didn't belong there."

His eyes narrowed as if he couldn't quite face what had happened there, then he touched her lips with the warmth of his fingers. "Shh, enough. That's the last thing I want to think about. All I want to think about is right now."

"Yes," she said, knowing she needed the same thing. As she slipped her hand lower, she skimmed over the soft trail of hair on his chest. She felt his breath catch as she moved lower until she felt the evidence of how much he wanted her. As much as she wanted him. And when she circled his strength with her hand, he groaned and pressed his head back into the mattress, his eyes closed.

"Oh, God, it's—" He took a shuddering breath, then moved abruptly.

His hands spanned her waist, and the next instant she was straddling him. With his dark eyes burning into hers, Quint eased her down on him until he filled her. It was both shocking and wonderful to her how right it felt. She looked down at him, into dark, fiery eyes, and knew she loved him in a way she had never loved another man in her life.

She felt as if he were a part of her, and when he started to move under her, feelings exploded in her. He was more than part of her, she thought as the pleasures mounted. Shards of joy shot through her, the momentum of their movements keeping pace with her building ecstasy.

When she felt the world explode into brilliant pleasure that left her breathless, when she heard Quint call her name, she knew that Quint was part of her soul.

QUINT NEVER SLEPT. He didn't want to waste time sleeping. Not when he was holding Annie, relishing her softness, her heat, lying in the gentle silence... and for the first time in an eternity, he wasn't alone.

Dreams in prison hadn't even come close to the reality of this woman. And nothing could come close to what he'd found when she gave herself to him. He closed his eyes, bombarded with emotions that he couldn't ever remember dealing with before.

Women had been there for him, some staying longer than others, but none had made him think about forever the way Annie did. A deep chill invaded his being as the word rang in his mind.

Forever. The pain radiating in him was unbearable as he admitted that there was no forever with this woman. Here and now was all he'd ever have of her.

Thoughts he'd had just before he touched Annie on the porch became clearer and more unavoidable. Annie wanted her child. She wanted stability and home and family and normalcy, and he knew that he couldn't give her any of those things. An ex-con was far from stable. He hadn't had a home for what seemed his entire life. His family consisted of one brother whom he saw every three or four years. And normalcy? Not even close.

When she stirred beside him, his body responded instantly to her contact. Forever would have never been long enough to be with Annie, but he knew he wasn't a man for forever. He never could be. What he had now was it, the sum total. He'd get Annie to her child, wish her well, then make himself walk away.

When she sighed softly, the sound ran havoc over his nerves. If he didn't get some distance from her right now, he'd never be able to let her go. If he took her one more time, the bond would grow even more, and breaking it would kill him.

Carefully, he eased away from her and got out of bed. For a moment, he let himself look down at her as she curled onto her side and settled back in sleep with a sigh. His hand moved as if of its own volition and almost touched her cheek, it almost brushed at her curls, but he drew back before he could let himself do it.

He made himself turn away and cross to the cupboard to get a sheet out of it, then he went back and covered Annie with the plain white cotton. She stirred, her hand clutched the linen and tugged it up under her chin. But she didn't awaken. The lashes lay in arcs against her translucent skin, her lips pale and softly parted.

The air was thin in here, and Quint felt as if the walls were closing in on him. He turned quickly and didn't look back as he went into the bathroom. But when he turned on the shower and stepped under the chilling cold water, nothing killed the desire in him for Annie.

As he was surrounded by cold, he knew that the life he'd thought he would lead alone had changed to a life he would lead being lonely. Wanting a woman he'd never have again and feeling as if he'd lost a part of himself. He couldn't change it. He had to live with it, but he wasn't at all sure how to do that.

Annie didn't remember drifting off, but one minute she was holding on to Quint, filled with his essence and touch, then she was coming out of a deep sleep with a light sheet over her. Quint was calling her name softly, "Annie? Annie?"

She slowly opened her eyes and rolled onto her back. He was over her at the side of the bed, shadows filling the room, but she could see his hair was damp and slicked back from his face in a low ponytail. And he'd dressed in a clean T-shirt and jeans. The mingled scent of freshness and soap permeated the air. He'd taken a shower without her knowing he'd left the bed. Yet she'd thought she would have sensed his leaving.

As she looked up at him and stretched her arms over her head, she froze. Something was wrong.

She struggled awkwardly to sit up and grabbed at a sheet Quint must have put over her. Had they been found, or were the police outside or coming up the drive? Or Trevor. "Quint, what's wrong?"

"Nothing, it's time to get up." The words were mundane and didn't fit that edge she felt at all.

Then Quint moved back a bit, and she could feel the withdrawal in action. The closeness that had been there, the intense joining before she'd slept, was gone. And it frightened her.

All she wanted right then was to touch him, to make some sort of connection, but she didn't. Instead, she added to the mundane words when she knew something monumental was happening. "What time is it?"

"Eight o'clock."

She felt confused and the need to see her daughter came with a vengeance. Sanity in her insanity. "We . . . we need to go," she said, clutching the sheet to her chest.

"I let you sleep as long as I could."

"Did...did you get some sleep?" she asked, desperate to get back that feeling of closeness, but not knowing how to do it.

"I'm fine." Then he said words that weren't mundane at all, words that made her eyes sting. "Time to get back to the real world. I guess this is over."

"Is it?" she breathed.

He studied her with darkly shadowed eyes. "Yes, it is. It has to be."

"But, I don't—"

He cut her off. "Get dressed and I'll take you to Sammi."

He moved farther back from her, almost receding into the gathering shadows of the room. He'd take her to Sammi. And something in her stopped her from asking "What then?" She didn't want to know that he'd leave her when he'd taken her to her daughter.

Something so right had changed, and she had no way to define it. She had made horrible mistakes in her life, but whatever was happening here, felt as if it could kill her. "Give me five minutes," she whispered, surprised that her voice sounded vaguely normal.

"I'll be outside," he said, then turned from her and crossed the room.

She didn't watch him step out the door. She didn't have to. She could feel the emptiness in the room as soon as he was gone, and she knew it was just the first version of the emptiness he'd leave behind if he left for good.

Pushing aside any thoughts except getting to Sammi, she got up and found her discarded clothes on the floor at the foot of the bed. Memories of how they were taken off shook her for a moment, then she picked up her things and dressed quickly. She didn't bother even looking in a mirror after tugging her hair back to catch it in a band. She put on her sandals, then looked around, found her suitcase and headed for the door.

But when she got to the entry, something made her turn and look back at the small, stark room. Hardly the setting to find out what love really was, what it felt like, what it could do to a person. Hardly the place of dreams, yet that's exactly what this room was until she woke from her sleep.

She glanced at the bed with its exposed mattress and the tangled sheet at the footboard. More memories flooded over her, and right then she heard Quint behind her.

"I'll take care of things in here and leave some money for the owner. Take your suitcase out to the car, and we can get out of here."

When he brushed by, she found herself holding her breath until he was well past and over by the bed. Then she looked at him as he grabbed the sheet and began to fold it. "Quint?"

"We don't have time to waste," he said as he finished with the sheet and crossed to the cupboard.

"But we—"

He turned, his expression hidden by the shadows in the room. "Annie, not now." His words were flat and abrupt.

Unapproachable. That was the only word she could come up with for this man. And it made her stomach ache. "Sure," she muttered, then turned and left.

She went out to the car, put her case in the back, then went around and got in. She felt as if she could barely breathe until Quint came out of the cabin. She didn't turn to watch him, and when he got in behind the wheel, she caught a glimpse of his hand closing over the gearshift out of the corner of her eye. Strong hands. Gentle hands. She looked away when she started to remember.

Silently, Quint drove the car back down the road to the chain, got out, took the chain down, then got back in and drove off without bothering to replace the barrier. By the time they got back to a main road, stars were spreading over the open sky, and a full moon was rising behind them.

She drove with a stranger she'd fallen in love with, a stranger who had shut her out as soon as she'd awakened. She stared out at the night as they headed down a two-lane road. The pavement climbed gradually until the air was thinner, and vast, dark fields on either side of the road were bordered by soaring mountains.

"I checked the map while you were asleep and found the best route to Taos," Quint finally said, the sound of his voice a jolt after the tense silence.

She felt uneasy with the idea of him being awake while she was asleep and with the idea that he covered her nakedness with the sheet. "Good," she murmured.

"We'll head due west and north about a hundred miles after the border. I don't know what the roads are like, but if we get very lucky, we'll be near Taos in four or five hours."

She let her head rest against the leather support, not able to bear making small talk right now. "That sounds like a plan."

"I guess it is."

She turned to Quint, who was a dark silhouette against the eerie glow from the dash. He was looking straight ahead. There was no way she could just pretend nothing happened, that she hadn't been touched by him or that he hadn't touched her soul. "Quint, what's going on?"

He checked the rearview mirror. "Nothing. We've got the road to ourselves for now."

"That isn't what I was talking about."

He never looked at her. "Then tell me what you're talking about."

"What happened back there?"

"We outran the police."

She wanted to scream, but she forced herself to keep her voice down. "No, at the cabin. You and me."

He looked in the side mirror, then regripped the steering wheel. "What do you want me to say?"

You love me, you want me, you want to see my child. "Nothing," she muttered.

"Hey, I didn't promise you anything. We had a good time. We enjoyed each other. That's it."

"That's it?" she echoed.

He was silent for such a long time that she was certain he wasn't going to answer her at all. Then she heard him exhale harshly. "What did you think it was?"

This was wrong, so wrong. "I don't know."

He slowed the car and glanced at her for the first time since they'd left the cabin. Night shadows hid his eyes, and she couldn't read his expression at all. "All right. Let's lay our cards out on the table. I wanted you back there, that was pretty obvious. I didn't plan it. It just happened."

Her hands were clenched so tightly that her nails were digging into her palms. "You can't mean that."

"Why not?"

"Quint, you can't... I mean, something like what happened between us isn't just some accident, some time out."

"That's exactly what it was. Something we both needed, but not something that lasts."

Each word twisted in her and the pain in her hands was a welcome diversion from other pain that ate at her. "How can you say something like that?"

"God, I was afraid of this happening."

"What?" she asked in a tight voice.

"It's my fault. I thought we both understood the ground rules."

"Stop," she whispered, enough was enough.

His glance touched her again, but this time she could see the set of his jaw. "There can't be any more. There isn't any more."

She held up one hand as if she could ward off the impact of his words. "How do you know that?"

"Take a good look at me and a good look at you. I've got a life waiting for me that doesn't have space for anyone else. I'm an ex-con. I'm on parole. Everything I've got is in this car, and when I hit my brother's place in Santa Barbara, the first place I have to go is to my parole officer. If I sneeze wrong, I'm back inside. It's a hell of a life for one person. And there's no room in it for anyone else."

"It doesn't have to be that way," she said. "It doesn't, I swear."

Quint could feel her looking at him, and he didn't know what to say to stop her and her words. His jaw clenched so tightly it ached, and his chest felt tighter. "It's what has to be."

"You won't give us a chance?"

"There is no 'us' to give a chance to," he said, hating the words even as he spoke them. There had never been an 'us' in his life, and suddenly he felt empty and very alone.

But one thought was there, and he needed to hold it up as a shield against every impulse that pummeled him. He was a dead end for Annie. And he wouldn't be anyone's dead end. Least of all hers. And that thought gave him words to say that were as ugly as any he'd heard in prison.

"I needed someone, anyone, and you were there. Is that clear enough for you?"

"You can't mean that," Annie choked. Pain was overwhelming. He'd used her. He'd taken her to satisfy some bottled up need. And she'd loved him. There weren't even any tears in her. Just the pain and the sure knowledge that she'd almost destroyed what life she had left.

"Sorry. You asked and I told you. It wasn't fair to you, but sometimes needs outrun good sense. And we've been alone. Do you have any idea what it's like to be cut off from everything, then to have it right there?"

"Stop it!" she gasped, fighting the need to press her hands to her ears to block out everything he was saying to her. "Just...just stop...please."

"You're right. Let's stop this right here."

Chapter Twelve

Annie looked out into the night and felt as if the darkness were invading her soul.

Quint moved abruptly, and for a moment she was terrified that he'd touch her. If he did, she'd surely hold on to him and never let go. But thankfully he was reaching for the radio. He turned it on, then sat back as the sounds of hard rock filled the empty spaces and cut off all talk.

The driving music beat against her senses, and she welcomed it, anything to distract her from the man next to her.

By the time Annie saw a glow of lights in the distance, they'd been in the state of New Mexico for two hours and her emotions had settled into a blessed stage of numbness. When a three-hour retrospective of the Rolling Stones started on the radio, Quint reached over and flipped the radio off.

"We'll gas up ahead, and you can make the phone call to Jeannie to let her know we're going to be there in a few hours."

It was a statement, not open to discussion, so Annie kept quiet as Quint drove toward the lights. When they got near, she could see that the glow came from a truck stop on the left side of the road. Brilliant neon lights lighted the sign by the road and outlined the roofs of a restaurant, a gas station and a repair garage. The land around the complex was bare of other buildings.

A half dozen diesel trucks idled to one side of a series of fuel pumps, and even though it was almost eleven o'clock, there was plenty of activity at the complex. She spotted a bank of telephones in a corner at the far end of the restaurant and picked up her purse to get change.

When Quint pulled in at the far end of the pumps and stopped, Annie scrambled out and, without a word to Quint, headed for a bank of pay phones by a row of newspaper stands in front of the restaurant. She didn't wait for Quint to say or do anything. There was nothing she wanted to hear from him, and if he drove off without her, she'd manage.

Only the need to hear Sammi's voice broke through her numbness, and she broke into a jog, passing two truckers who were exiting the restaurant. She picked the last phone in the line, the one closest to a jutting wall so no one could come up behind her without her seeing them. Laying her coins on the side counter, she put in the call, then deposited the money the operator asked for.

The phone rang twice before Jeannie answered it.

"Hello?"

"Jeannie, it's me, I've—"

"Listen, I told you before I can't come in tonight. It's too late. I don't care what's going on."

Annie closed her eyes tightly and any numbness she'd used in the car to salvage her sanity was slipping away. "Oh, God, is Trevor there? Did he manage to—"

"No," Jeannie said immediately.

"Someone he sent?"

"Now you're getting it."

Annie held the phone so tightly she was sure the plastic would snap. "What about Sammi?"

"That's not the problem. My husband's not here, and I can't just leave. You'll just have to close up the restaurant on your own."

"Jeannie, is Sammi all right?"

"Absolutely."

"Does Trevor know where she is?"

"Not at all."

"Is she with Charlie?" she asked.

"Yes."

She pressed a hand over her eyes. "All right. I'm in New Mexico, a couple of hours from Taos."

"That's good."

"We need to meet where Trevor won't look. Not the restaurant...uh..." Then she knew. Jeannie and Chuck had a house they kept north of the city in a high valley. It was isolated and there was no way Trevor could know about it. "Los Olivos," she whispered. They'd named the place after an ancient olive tree in the courtyard of the house.

"That sounds like a good compromise."

"I'll get there as soon as I can. Wait for me and don't let Sammi out of your sight."

Jeannie spoke quickly. "I don't have time for this. I'll see you there when I can manage it." And the line clicked.

Annie slowly hung the phone back on the hook, then leaned against the wide wall of the building. The flashing lights from the neon signs gave a garish glow to everything around her, making it feel as surreal as she felt right now. Trevor had sent someone to get Sammi, and he wouldn't be far behind.

"What's going on?" Quint asked from close by.

Startled, Annie spun around and he was there, tall and strong and in control. And she wished he was there for her. But he wasn't. He'd made it clear that he never would be after he dropped her off. She was in this alone. A few days ago, it would have been what she expected, but now she felt as if she weren't anchored, as if she could fall apart.

"He did it," she said.

"Trevor?"

She bit her lip hard and nodded.

"What did he do?"

"He sent someone to Jeannie's to get Sammi." She hugged her arms around herself and dug her fingers into her upper arms, welcoming the slight pain to keep her focused. "He's there now."

Quint hated the pain he could see in Annie's expression. Her mouth was tight, her skin pale, and that unsteadiness in her chin was there again. Then she wrapped her arms around herself and it struck a chord in him that he could barely deal with. Holding herself together, always having to keep things under control.

She was terrified, and touching her was a need deep in his soul. But he couldn't, or he'd be back to square one. "Then you'll have to come up with an alternative place to meet your friend," he said with as much cool logic as he could muster.

She met his gaze, but her look was almost empty, as if she'd turned in on herself, and there was no connection. He should have been thankful to have the intensity broken, but it only made him more edgy.

"We found a place. Jeannie and Charlie have a second home in the mountains north of the city. Trevor would have no way of knowing about it. You can drop me at the Pennington turnoff this side of Taos, and I'll get a ride from there."

He'd never just "drop her," but he wasn't going to argue with her right now. "Let's go. We've a two hour drive ahead of us."

She nodded, then turned, scooped up some change on the shelf by the phone and brushed past him, stirring the night air, but not touching him. He took a steadying breath before heading after her.

THE TENSION IN THE CAR was palpable by the time Quint spotted a sign that said they were fifty miles from Taos. His nerves were frayed, and he needed to hear voices, something to fill the void. "Who was at Jeannie's when you called?"

Annie stirred as if his speaking startled her. Then she said, "Pardon me?"

"When you called Jeannie, you said someone was there. I asked who it was."

"Oh, I don't know," she sighed. "A flunky of Trevor's, probably an attorney, or maybe someone who owes him or the family."

"Where's your daughter?"

"She's with Charlie, and I hope to God whomever Trevor sent doesn't catch up to them. Quint, she's so little, and she doesn't deserve what Trevor's doing."

Words meant to fill spaces were only making things worse. He looked at Annie huddled in her seat with her back to the door, staring at her hands clenched in her lap. "Most of us don't deserve what we get," he said.

"Or don't get what we deserve," she said. "I've heard about mothers who've killed someone who'd threatened their children. I never thought I could do that, but now I know I could."

"Let's hope it doesn't come to that," he murmured. "Juries seldom understand passion or truth in a defense."

She shifted and he knew that she was looking at him now. "When you told them the truth, they didn't believe you, did they?"

"A jury never heard my story. I beat the hell out of the guy, so I couldn't claim I was innocent, and they only had my word about why I did it. I opted for a plea bargain."

"Why? Maybe a jury—"

"Did I tell you who the guy was that I found raping that girl?"

"No."

"Gerald Darling, a talk show host in the Boston area. He's a downright saint in those parts. I worked for him for six months and he wasn't even close to being a saint. He's a drug addict, mean as horse manure and usually takes whatever he wants to take.

"But if I'd gone in front of a jury, twelve good people would have listened to him declaring his innocence, backed by a woman who swore she was involved with him because she wanted to be. I'd have come off as a lout who went crazy, beat the man half to death, then tried to cover my tracks by claiming I thought she was being raped."

"Maybe they would have been smart enough to see through his lies."

"Image is his business, and he's damned good at it."

"But you don't have a record, do you?"

"Years back I was known to take care of myself, and I've had my share of run-ins with the law. But nothing major." He laughed roughly. "Terminal stupidity, I guess it was always there."

"You should have taken the chance at a trial."

"If I'd gone to trial for attempted murder, the charge the D.A. was going to push, I could have gotten twenty to life instead of five years, no matter what my past was. I figured I could take anything for two years, if I got good time."

"But you lost two years of your life."

What life? he thought, but merely said, "Actually, it was almost worth it to see Darling lying on the ground grabbing for his teeth."

"There wasn't anyone who'd back you up or help?"

"I didn't have a Jeannie and Charlie in my life, just my attorney and he was paid well for it. He got most of my money."

"What happened to Darling?"

"According to my well-paid attorney, he went into a rehab program very quietly about two months after the incident, and he's still got his talk show." He exhaled harshly. "Actually, I'd be in the television room at the prison and there he'd be, up on the screen, smiling and talking and having a life."

"It must have been awful for you."

"It was passable. There were other things to worry about inside than Darling out there having a good time. I learned that you get through by living your life and letting others lead theirs. That's all you can do."

"You didn't do that when you tried to stop that man from raping the woman."

"Look where it got me."

"So you just isolate yourself?"

"I live my life," he muttered, hating the way she was throwing his own words back at him. "That's all I can handle, and sometimes I don't handle that very well."

Annie knew the feeling. The numbness had been slipping since she left the gas station, and now it was all but gone. As Quint spoke, she felt as if she were one raw nerve. "Most of us don't handle life very well, but we try."

"And you survive?"

"I try."

"What about before you met Trevor Raines, what was your life like?"

She was edgy, and the words were a diversion for her, a way to keep from facing her problems in silence. And talking about her past seemed safe. She could barely remember that life, and it didn't have the edges to it that talking about the present had.

"I was an only child, and when my parents died I was seventeen. They left enough for me to get by if I didn't need anything past the necessities. I graduated from high school a year early, but I couldn't manage college, so I went to work . . . waitressing, clerking, whatever I could find.

"When I got to Taos, I applied for a job at the restaurant, and the rest, as they say, is history."

"Then you met Trevor Raines?"

"Yes, and he seemed like fun, like he didn't have a care in the world, and I fell for it. And when he came back two months ago, I was exhausted from worrying and trying to make things work." That girl had been so tired of being alone and trying to make things work for herself. "And he offered a life that seemed so good. It would have been wonderful for Sammi. She would have had everything."

"But it blew up in your face."

She could feel her stomach knotting. "I was stupid and gullible."

"And you did what you thought you had to do."

"So did you."

"You can't compare what I've done with my life with what you've done in your life."

"We both waded in, thinking we were doing the best thing."

"Random acts of mindless stupidity."

"I guess so."

"After you get Sammi, what then?"

"I don't know. I'll have to figure it out as I go along. I've got a bit of money saved. And my car . . ." She sighed as she remembered the last glimpse she had of her car nose down in the ditch. "I'll figure it out."

"I've been thinking about your car."

"What about it?"

"Why don't you let me help you out?"

"What?"

"You went off the road because of me, so why not let me give you some money to help out? I didn't spend anything in prison, and the lawyer left some of it intact."

He was serious. "I wasn't watching and pulled out in front of you. That's hardly your fault. I should be thanking you for not hitting me right then."

"But you need—"

"No, I don't need your money." She turned away from him. "I don't want it."

"I was just trying to help."

"I know what you were doing."

"What's that?"

She looked back at him. "You've made it really clear that what happened between us was a lapse in sanity. That's enough. You don't have to salve your conscience by paying me. That would make me feel like a . . . a . . ." She almost choked on the word.

"Like what?" he demanded, his voice low and tight.

"You know."

"Yeah, I do, and believe me, I didn't mean it that way. If I wanted to pay for sex, I would have hit a whorehouse when I got out. Twenty bucks and no conscience. The perfect solution, if that's what I was looking for."

Annie turned from the sight of him, her face flaming as she absorbed his words. And even worse was the fact that she felt physically sick at the thought of Quint being with another woman, even a prostitute. But the horrible truth was she had no right feeling anything like that. There would surely be a lot of women in his life, and she wasn't going to be one of them.

She felt the car's speed increase, then looked around and realized that Quint had turned off the main highway and headed north. "What are you doing?" she said as she looked back at Quint.

The night was a great shield, saving her from meeting his gaze head-on. "I'm driving?"

"Where? Taos is west, not north."

"You said you were heading north at the Pennington interchange. Well, we just hit it and we're going north."

"No, not us. I'm going north, not you."

"My car, my rules. I'll take you to your friend's house then I'll drop you. Now, tell me where I'm going."

She felt drained and there wasn't anything left in her to fight Quint. Then without warning, lightning cut through the sky, crashing with forked fury into the land to the north and bathing the world in a flash of pale light.

"How far do we have to go?" Quint asked.

"Eight or nine miles," she said as the world settled back into the darkness of night.

"We've got time before the storm breaks," he said and she felt the car speed up.

She looked ahead at the road where it cut into a high valley, with mountains on either side and grassy grazing land framing the road. And she couldn't believe that they were so close to success. She stared into the night and when another lightning bolt ripped across the heavens, she flinched.

She felt fragmented, filled with excitement and joy in one part, to be so close to seeing Sammi again, to holding her and knowing she was all hers. Yet there was an ache deep inside her, too, when she thought about Quint walking out of her life in a short time. She was going to miss him, not the man who'd turned from her, but the man who had held her and made love to her at the cabin.

She cut off those thoughts when she recognized the land, the scrub oak and aspens, then they rounded a corner and she spotted the road that led to Jeannie's house.

"Turn right there," she said.

As Quint slowed the car and turned onto the lane that climbed higher, it started to rain. The drops were large and scattered, and a cool breeze started to build.

"How far is it?" he asked.

"Right at the top of the hill."

She felt the car's back tires spin as the rain began to form a thin layer of slick water on the pavement, then traction was there and the car took the steep hill easily.

As they crested the top of the road, a bolt of lightning rocked the land, and its pale light exposed the house and the area around it. The single-story structure looked like a Spanish hacienda, fashioned of dark wood, adobe brick and a red clay tile roof. The veranda stretched the length of the house, supported by dark wooden posts set in terra-cotta tile, and there wasn't a light on in the whole house.

As lightning crashed around them again, the rain began to come down in torrents and Annie sat forward. She was getting drenched, but she didn't care. As soon as Quint stopped the car on the drive by the triple car garage, Annie scrambled out and ran for the front door.

She heard Quint yell after her, "I'll put the top up and get your bag," but she didn't stop. She went up the tiled steps and hurried to the door. As rain beat down on the land, Annie grabbed the door and turned the knob. But it didn't give. The house was locked up tight. She backed up, looking up and down the front of the house, then went back to the door and hit it with her fist.

"Jeannie! Jeannie! It's me!" she screamed, but nothing stirred behind the barrier.

"Haven't they gotten here?" Quint said from behind her.

She pressed her forehead to the door and closed her eyes tightly. "They had an hour's drive, and it's been three hours since I talked to Jeannie." She swallowed hard. "They should be here. But...but they...they aren't. No one's here."

"Annie, there's any number of reasons why they're late that have nothing to do with Trevor."

She turned, tears mingling with the rain on her face. "He found her, Quint. Trevor got Sammi."

A flash of lightning shot from the sky behind Quint, making a stark silhouette out of the man. He was drenched, with his T-shirt molded to his chest and shoulders and his hair pressed against his head. She couldn't see his face at all in the stark contrast of light and dark.

"You don't know that for sure. Anything could have happened. So, first thing, we go in the house and if they have their phone connected, we can call their place. If they don't, I'll go back to find a pay phone and call."

"I don't have a key. I thought they'd be here." She was shivering from nerves and the chill of the rain. "They sh-should..."

Quint moved past her, took something out of his pocket, and when she turned, she saw the door swing silently open. Quint pushed something in his pocket and said, "Don't ask. Just accept the fact the door's open. Now, come on inside out of the rain."

She hurried past him into the house and felt for the light switch on the wall. She flipped it up, and a light by a dark leather couch beside an adobe fireplace flashed on. Its low light touched the large living room with just enough light to see the phone on the table by the couch.

Annie hurried over to the phone on an end table by the couch and grabbed the receiver. She stopped when she saw a red light flashing frantically on the answering machine sitting by it.

Quint came up behind her, then reached past her to press the "Play" button. As he drew back, a computerized voice said, "You have one message." A beep sounded, then Jeannie's voice came on.

"Had a problem, but it's settled, and we're on our way. Stay by the phone. We'll be there in an hour." The beep sounded, then the monotone voice said the date and time. They'd missed Jeannie's call by four minutes.

"Oh, God," Annie said, burying her face in her hands, her relief so great that she could feel her legs giving way. The next thing she knew, Quint had her in his arms, holding her to him, and she let herself lean on him. "She's on her way," she whispered against the damp heat of his chest.

"Yes, she is, and it's all going to be all right for you."

Even as she heard his words, she knew how wrong he was. Sammi would get here and she was more than thankful for that, but everything wouldn't be all right. Not as long as he was leaving. She tipped her head back and looked up into his face.

This was all she'd ever have. The memory of him holding her, the scent of rain and maleness clinging to him, and she wanted so much more. So very much more. So she took a gamble, and stood on tiptoe to touch her lips to his. At first he didn't respond and she was afraid he'd set her back and let her go.

But he didn't break the contact. With a low groan that echoed deep inside her, he pulled her to him. There was no gentle taking in Quint's touch, no patience, no leisurely building of passion. The aching need and burning desire were there instantly, white-hot and all consuming. Without a moment of hesitation, she gave in to it.

With every touch, every contact, she felt the man burning his imprint in her soul, a remembrance for her so she'd never forget this man. It didn't matter to her why he was doing this, all that mattered was he was here, and she knew that he wanted her as much as she wanted him.

His hands worked their way under her damp top, frantically pushing aside the clinging cotton until he was touching her breasts. She shuddered and almost cried out from the intensity of the sensations. Arching to him, she ached for more, hating the barrier of clothing that was stopping skin to skin contact.

Awkwardly she tugged at his T-shirt, trying to peel the damp material from his skin. He let her go and skimmed off his shirt, dropping it at their feet. She stood facing him, in the low light never breaking eye contact with him, then very deliberately pulled off her own top.

There was no embarrassment in her when the material fell away exposing her to his gaze. Her nipples tightened, and her stomach ached. To want a man so completely was new to her, unique, and so was the pain when she thought that this would be the very last time.

"God, you're beautiful," he said, his voice low and rasping. Then he reached out and cupped her breasts in his hands, but he never looked away from her. "We can't...not here, not when your friends..."

"They won't be here for over half an hour," she said, her voice unsteady with emotion.

He looked around. "Where?"

She took him by the hand and led him across the room into a shadowy hallway. Then she opened the first door they came to and stepped into a tiny bedroom. Lightning struck outside and lighted the small room for a flashing moment as Annie turned to Quint.

"Please," she whispered as she reached for the top button of his jeans. "One last time."

Chapter Thirteen

"Yes," Quint whispered on a shudder as she lowered his zipper. Then Annie felt him with her hands, relishing his response to her, and the hissing breath he took when she moved slowly on him.

"Enough," he rasped as his breath seemed to catch in his throat. Then he let her go to push off his denims and step out of them.

When he hooked his finger in the top button of her shorts, she stood very still. His eyes never left hers as he eased the button out of its loop, then skimmed the cotton down over her hips until it fell around her ankles. His sure fingers found the elastic of her panties, and in one smooth motion, they fell on top of her shorts, then she stepped out of both of them.

She lifted her hand and rested it on Quint's chest. As lightning slashed through the skies and rain drove against the windows, she felt his heart beating against her palm. And his stark image washed in the flash of the electric jolt seared into her mind.

When the room faded into darkness again, Quint eased Annie back until they both fell onto the coolness of the comforter on the bed. Side by side, they explored each other, their hands skimming over damp skin, finding places of pleasure.

Quint traced the swelling of Annie's hip, then splayed his fingers on her stomach. As his touch went lower, Annie held her breath and waited. Then he touched her, the heel of his hand pressed against her, and as he slowly moved in circles, she felt as if the energy of the electrical storm outside was shooting through her. The sensations rode one on top of the next until she thought she would explode from pleasure.

When she was sure the aching pleasure would fragment her, Quint was over her and his strength, silky and hot, was against her, testing her. And when she couldn't bear it any more, she begged him to take her, and he eased himself into her. He filled her, deeply and surely, and when he didn't move, Annie opened her eyes and looked up at him over her.

His hair fell forward, and she could see the sheen of moisture on his skin. She loved him. She wanted to tell him, to hear the words said out loud just this once, but she couldn't take the chance. She couldn't bear to have him leave her, to walk away now. Not yet.

So instead she began to move her hips and on a shudder, he moved with her to match her rhythm. She lost herself in brilliant feelings, the friction between them building the pleasure to a level that seemed surreal.

Then in a moment of pure sensations, when the world was transformed into a place for just the two of them, she let herself go. Right then, it went beyond anything she'd ever experienced before, and Annie knew that no matter what she had left when this was over, it was well worth it to love Quint one last time.

As his feelings began to settle into a mellow satisfaction, Quint held Annie to him in the tiny bedroom but neither person slept. There wasn't time to settle in and just enjoy the lingering feelings. No time at all. When the storm rumbled outside, he knew it was an echo of what was going on inside himself. As lightning crashed, the naked light lighted the world and he made himself shift away from Annie.

He didn't look back at her as he stood by the bed and found his jeans, then tugged them on. They were cold and damp and their feeling, as he pushed his legs into them, was a help. Then he turned and looked at Annie sitting up in bed, naked, watching him. As he did up the zipper, he turned away from the sight of her. Even with the wet, cold denim on, he could feel a response to her coming again.

"I'll get your bag out of the car," he said over his shoulder and left the bedroom to go back through the house and out the front door into the rain.

By the time he got back with the luggage and a change of clothes for himself, he was wet again and Annie was in the living room wearing a navy terry cloth robe that looked ten sizes too big for her. But thankfully it covered her from her neck to her calves.

She tugged at the tie at her waist. "I think this is Charlie's. I found it in their room."

He put her bag on the floor, then held up his duffel bag. "Where can I change?"

She motioned behind her with her head. "The room. Use it."

Annie moved to one side, and they made no contact, not even eye contact as he went past her into the hallway. She waited until she heard the door to the bedroom close, then she released a breath that she'd been holding.

She hugged her arms around herself, then crossed to the front windows and stared out at the night being torn by the lightning from the storm. The rain finally stopped, but the lightning persisted, and every bolt of electricity seemed to rip through her.

What she found with Quint was full and complete, but as soon as he moved away from her, she felt fragmented again. And no matter how she hugged her arms around herself, nothing made her feel whole. Not the way she felt when she was in Quint's arms.

Lightning ripped through the heavens again, then the world went black outside at the same time she saw a light down the driveway. Then it grew and she knew they'd made it. "They're here!" she yelled as she ran for the door and flicked on the porch lights.

She heard him come running into the room, and she looked back as she grabbed the doorknob. He was in fresh clothes, a dark T-shirt and dry jeans, but his feet were bare and his hair loose. "They're here. They made it."

She pulled the door open and went out onto the porch, soft yellow light barely penetrating the darkness around the house. She stayed in the shelter of the overhang and watched the car come closer. But it wasn't Jeannie's car, and for a horrifying second she thought she was standing there in the light while Trevor, or someone he'd sent, was coming to the house.

There was no point in going inside and hiding, so she stood there by the steps and prayed that it wasn't Trevor. The car stopped by the Corvette, the engine stilled and the headlights clicked off, then a man got out of the driver's side.

Her prayers were answered. "Charlie!" she called as the man turned to look at her on the porch.

He waved, then hurried around the car and opened the back passenger side door. He ducked inside, then came out carrying Sammi snuggled into his shoulder. Not caring that her feet were bare or the ground was cold and wet, Annie ran down the steps and met Charlie halfway between the drive and the house.

"Oh, Sammi," she said as she took her sleepy daughter in her arms. When the baby's arms went around her neck, Annie felt a dark void that had been in her disappear, and she knew that this made everything she'd been through worth it. Everything.

Quint stood in the doorway and watched from a distance. He saw a tall, thin man get out of the car then hurry around and go to the back to take out the child. He had a flashing glimpse of Sammi before Annie had her in a tight hug, a tiny, towheaded child. Then a woman got out of the passenger side and hurried over to Annie.

Jeannie and Charlie . . . and Samantha. He watched them as Jeannie urged Annie back to the house, helping her avoid puddles on the ground. "It's too damp out here for the two of you," she said.

Quint backed up a bit as the group came toward the house and into the glow of the porch lights, then up the steps. Jeannie was tiny, with dark hair, and a quick, urgent way of moving. She was dressed in dark pants and a light sweatshirt. Charlie, thin and ambling, wearing chinos and a polo shirt, seemed to be hovering over the two women and the child.

"I'm Annie's ride," Quint said as both people paused at the top of the steps and looked at him.

Jeannie smiled, then moved toward him with her hand outstretched. "I'm Jeannie and this is my husband Charlie. Thank you for everything you've done for our Annie," she said as she shook his hand.

"No problem."

Then Annie was there with Samantha in her arms. If Quint had been asked to pick Annie's child out of a crowd of other children, he would have chosen Sammi right away. She was tiny and delicate, with a fine, silky cap of pale hair that curled softly around her ears and at her neck. Her sleepy face had a tiny nose with a brush of freckles, and eyes the color of her mother's.

She looked up at Quint but never let go of her hold on her mother or took her head off Annie's shoulder. Then she frowned at him. "Mommy? Man?"

"Yes, this is Quint."

"Kint," she repeated solemnly.

"Quint," Annie said softly as she looked at Quint, her face tear streaked but beautifully touched with a happiness he wished he'd put there. "This is my Samantha, but anyone who knows her calls her Sammi."

He looked from Annie to the child. "Hi, Sammi," he said, and she gave him a smile that showed a faint dimple on her right cheek.

He moved to one side to let the people pass into the house, but he was dealing with another experience he'd never had before. He accepted the fact that he'd fallen irrevocably in love with Annie. He accepted that as a done deal, something he'd have to live with. But he'd never dreamed he'd look at her child and feel a connection that came from nowhere.

He watched them go to the couch and chairs and settle in front of the hearth. How could it be possible? Both the mother and the child had some sort of secret weapon that went straight to his heart and he didn't have any idea what it was. All he knew was that it was there, and it was producing an insanity in him that was making him start to think of things that couldn't possibly be. That shouldn't be.

He moved into the room and closed the door, but didn't go closer to the others. He stood by the windows with his back to the night and couldn't take his eyes off Annie and the baby.

On the couch, Annie held Sammi on her lap, and as the baby snuggled into her, Annie stroked her silky hair. Charlie settled in one of the chairs and Jeannie went toward a doorway on the right. "I'm making coffee. Any takers?" she called over her shoulder.

"Make a pot," Charlie said. "We all need it." He smiled at the baby in Annie's arms as he settled with his legs stretched out and his hands resting on the chair arms. "She's something. Never complained a bit. Did what we asked. She's a doll."

When Quint saw Annie press a kiss to her daughter's head, he turned to look out the window at a darkness he'd have to go out into alone.

He heard Annie speaking. "She's a doll, all right. Now, tell me what happened?" Charlie must have motioned to Quint because Annie said, "Quint knows everything. He's the only reason I'm here right now. Without him . . ." He heard her sigh and he closed his eyes as she continued. "Let's just say that he got me here. You can say anything in front of him that you'd say to me."

"All right, that's good enough for me," Charlie said. "I'd taken the baby to the park for a break, and when I got near the house when we were going home, I saw a car parked in the driveway. I didn't recognize it, and something stopped me from going home. I guess I figured that Trevor would pull something.

"So, I headed in the opposite direction and got to a phone to call Jeannie. She let me know not to come back, so I told her I was going to Sandy's—our bookkeeper—and we waited there until Jeannie could call me.

"I guess the guy stayed for a long time, then sat out in front of the house for two hours. Jeannie finally called and we decided to meet at Sandy's, then head out from there. We didn't want to take the chance that they'd know our car, so we borrowed Sandy's." He exhaled harshly. "Damn, I felt like I was in some sort of James Bond movie."

"This isn't make-believe, Charlie. Trevor wants Sammi so he won't lose his inheritance. That's the only reason."

"We figured it had to be something pretty serious for you to take off like that."

"Here's hot coffee for everyone," Jeannie said, and Quint turned as she came into the room with a tray holding a coffeepot and four mugs. "I didn't buy what that guy Trevor sent was saying, either. He was trying to tell us that you attacked Trevor, that he was desperate to find you. He wanted to take the baby back to the ranch so she'd be safe, and if you came back, then she'd be there. It sounded so... out of character for Trevor to worry about anyone but himself."

"You never liked him?" Annie asked with a touch of surprise in her voice.

"No, but I bit my lip. I knew you thought you were doing the right thing." Jeannie put the tray on the table in front of the couch, then looked at Sammi. "She's asleep again. Do you want to put her down in the back bedroom?"

"No," Annie said quickly. "I never want her to be out of my sight again. She can sleep here for now." Annie eased the child down onto the couch and Sammi stirred.

She opened her eyes and held out her hand to her mother. "Hand, peeze," she whispered, and Annie took the child's hand in hers. As soon as the contact was made, Sammi settled back into sleep.

Quint looked at the tiny fingers wrapped around Annie's. A connection. A connection of the heart. He looked at Charlie, who was pouring coffee into the mugs.

"Want some?" Charlie asked him.

Quint shook his head. "I need to get going."

Annie looked at him. "You can't."

He braced himself, then met her gaze. "I have to."

"Quint, you need to lay low."

He almost smiled at that expression. "What?"

"You know, get out of sight, stop and wait until you've got a chance to get past the law."

"Yes, I know," he said softly.

"Then you have to know that you need to stay out of sight for a while longer. They know your car. They'll be looking for it, and I'm sure you don't want to leave without that car."

"I can't stay."

She kept her hold on her daughter's hand. "Quint. Just stay long enough to rest and find out the best way to make it out of New Mexico. Charlie can help you. He travels all over the state."

He knew he should grab his things and leave, but everything had begun to shift for him. What had seemed an absolute before they got here had changed. And he wasn't sure when it happened. He looked at Annie and actually wondered "what if." What if he stayed? What if he tried to give her a life, a good life for her and the baby? A "stupidity response," maybe, but part of him wanted to try.

Maybe if he stayed a bit longer he could figure out what was the best thing to do. "I am tired."

Charlie stood. "Then it's settled. You can stay here as long as you need to."

"Thanks," he said.

"Come and I'll show you to your room."

Quint nodded. "Thanks," he replied and crossed to follow Charlie into the hallway, but Charlie passed the door of the room Quint and Annie had been in earlier. He stopped by a closed door on the opposite side of the hallway and looked at Quint. "Just one thing?"

"What's that?"

"I don't know what's going on between you and Annie, but I want you to know that she's like family to Jeannie and me. She's been through more than enough for any one person to take."

"Yes, I know," Quint said.

"I'd hate to see her get hurt."

"Me, too."

"Good, we both want the same thing."

"It looks that way," Quint said.

"Then you're very welcome here." He opened the door and stood back. "Get some rest."

Quint went into the darkened room and closed the door behind him. The room was small and for a moment, Quint felt as if he couldn't quite breathe. His lungs were tight and the air seemed thin. But it had nothing to do with the altitude. He crossed to heavy drapes on the far wall, pulled them back, then slid the window open. As he drew cool, rain-fresh air into his lungs, he watched lightning far off in the distance cut jagged forks in the night.

He should have gone. He should be in the car now and leaving this all behind. But no matter what he'd thought he could do, he couldn't leave. He pressed his hand flat on the glass and knew that he was either in the process of destroying his life, or he was finding a life he never suspected he could have.

ANNIE SLEPT WITH SAMMI that night in the room she'd shared so briefly with Quint. She held her daughter close, listening to her soft breathing and relishing her closeness. But she listened for other sounds, too. Something in her fully expected to hear a bedroom door open and close, then the front door open and close, and the Corvette start and drive off. But there were only night sounds when Annie finally fell asleep.

She woke when she felt something hit her in the stomach, something soft and small, and when she opened her eyes Sammi was sitting up beside her. A furry ball was lying on Annie's stomach. "Mommy, up, up."

Annie smiled at her daughter and held out her arms. "I'll get up, but first Mommy needs a big hug," she said.

Sammi fell into her arms. When she thought about what Trevor could rob her of, it made her heart ache. "Mommy loves Sammi," she whispered unsteadily.

"Me, too," a little voice piped up.

Annie held Sammi back and smiled up at her. "What did you say?"

Sammi smiled at her. "Me, too. Me, too. Me, too," she chanted as she wiggled to get free of Annie's hold. She squirmed free and stood in the middle of the bed. "Mommy, come, come."

When Annie sat up, Sammi scrambled back, shinnied off the bed and she ran for the door. "Hey, you, don't go out until Mommy gets up."

Sammi stretched to try to reach the knob, but she could barely touch it with the tips of her fingers. She turned to Annie who was slipping out of bed. "Peeeze, peeze, open, Mommy, open."

Annie grabbed the navy robe and slipped it on while she crossed to the door. "Are you hungry?"

"Huh," Sammi said with a nod of her head.

"Good." She put out her hand and Sammi took it. But Annie wasn't hungry. She was tense and almost afraid to go out in case she'd missed Quint leaving and she'd see the Corvette was gone.

"Fooot Woops," Sammi said as Annie opened the door.

"I don't know if Jeannie will have Froot Loops, but I bet she's got Cheerios."

"Fooot Woops, Fooot Woops," Sammi chanted as they went down the hallway to the kitchen.

When Annie stepped into the kitchen, Jeannie was already there and miraculously had a box of Froot Loops on the table. Annie smiled at her. "You remembered Froot Loops."

"I grabbed a few things before I left. Top of the list was the Froot Loops, number one survival ration."

Sammi ran across the Mexican tiled floor and threw herself at Jeannie, wrapping her arms around the woman's legs. "Fooot Woops, peeeze."

"Yes, sweet, you can have some," Jeannie said and picked up Sammi to slip her onto a wicker chair at the glass-topped table. She took a handful of the cereal out of the box and laid it on the table. "Help yourself while I get a bowl and some milk."

While Sammi picked out the pink ones, Jeannie looked at Annie and both women looked dead serious. "You're going to have to leave, aren't you?"

Annie nodded. "I'm afraid so. I hate to, but Trevor won't stop until we're back together or he's got me in jail."

"I know. I figured as much, but I hate to see the two of you going off alone." She looked at Sammi who was totally involved in making a small pile out of all the pink Froot Loops. "What about the man who brought you here?"

"Quint?"

"Was there more than one?"

Annie couldn't muster a smile. There was only one Quint in this world. "Just Quint."

"What's the story with him? You sounded pretty frantic on the phone."

"He's the only reason I made it this far. He beat up a trucker who was making a pass at me, and he outran the police."

Jeannie was getting a bowl out of the cupboard, and she stopped to look back at Annie. "He what?"

"Trevor got the state troopers after me. Now Quint's in trouble because he's been with me and they've got a make on his car."

She put the bowl on the table and crossed to the refrigerator. "So, what's his stake in all of this if he's put himself on the line like that?"

"He was coming this way, and—"

Jeannie carried milk over to the table. "He just happened to get in a fight and just happened to evade arrest?"

Annie wrapped the tie of the robe around and around her finger. "Jeannie, I can't talk about this now. But I need to see him. Is he still here?"

As Jeannie made a dish of cereal for Sammi, she said, "He and Charlie were out on the porch last time I looked." Annie's relief was overwhelming. Quint was still here. "For what it's worth," Jeannie said, "Charlie likes him."

"That's easy to do," Annie said.

"What's easy to do?" Quint asked from behind her.

Annie closed her eyes to try to center herself, then she turned to Quint. She couldn't look at him without her heart racing and her mouth going dry. He was in the doorway to the room, dressed in a dark T-shirt and jeans, and his hair was pulled back from his face.

"Good morning," she said softly.

He met Annie's gaze for a long moment, then said, "I'm glad you're up." But before she could ask why, Sammi spotted him.

"Kint, see Sammi's Fooot Woops."

He looked past her at the child and his expression was unreadable. She didn't know what she'd hoped for, maybe that he'd take one look at Sammi and fall in love, or maybe at least look as if he were put off by her presence.

"Fooot Woops?" he asked.

"Dis," Sammi said earnestly and held up a handful of the pink pieces.

"Oh, cereal."

"Huh," the baby said.

"It's her favorite," Annie said.

His dark eyes came back to her. "Can we talk somewhere?"

She hesitated, but didn't have an out when Jeannie cut in. "Go and talk. I'll make sure Sammi gets fed."

Annie fiddled with the tie on her robe again. "Let me get dressed, and we can talk," she murmured, then went past Quint without looking at him again.

ANNIE HURRIED BACK down the hall to the bedroom and went in where she could take a deep, calming breath. She dressed quickly into jeans and a loose white shirt, then went back down the hall. As she stepped into the kitchen, she stopped in the doorway.

Sammi and Quint were at the table, and on the glass top in front of them, the cereal had been segregated into piles according to color. Quint was arranging all the red pieces in a circle.

"Red," Sammi said and clapped her hands.

"Excellent," Quint said.

The vision of the tiny towheaded child with the lean dark man looked too appealing to Annie, and too right. She steeled herself against the dreams that came without warning. Don't dream, she told herself. Don't do that to yourself. Not now. Not here. Not with Quint.

Chapter Fourteen

"Quint?" Annie finally managed to say.

He spoke softly to Sammi. "Thanks for letting me do the reds," he said as he patted her head, then he got up and turned to Annie. "Outside?" he asked.

"Sure." She nodded and led the way into the living room and across to French doors on the side wall. She could sense Quint behind her, and when she stepped out onto the clay-tiled terrace, she stopped in the shade of the ancient olive tree.

When she turned to face Quint who stood by the doors in the bright sunlight, she knew without a doubt that what he was going to say would change her life forever. She clasped her hands in front of her and waited. Whatever happened, she knew she couldn't change it. This was Quint's decision.

Quint stood by the doors, then turned and closed them before turning back to Annie. The sun was warm, but the breeze kept it from being hot. The thin air of the high altitude was fresh and touched with a blossom sweetness that he couldn't place. But nothing was sweeter than the sight of Annie three feet from him in the partial shade of the olive tree.

The night had been long and one not given to sleep. It had been almost dawn before he finally knew what he was going to do. His choices were to drive away, leave this all behind and hope Annie found everything she wanted with someone else. The second choice was to bring her out here and tell her that he loved her and that he'd do whatever it took to make her and Sammi happy.

When it came right down to it, he knew as he looked at her, that he really didn't have a choice.

"I didn't know if you'd be here when I got up," Annie said. A slight paleness touched her skin, and her eyes were partially hidden by the lacy shade of her lashes. "I expected to find you gone."

"I thought about it," he said with all honesty. "But I couldn't just take off, not any more than I could have taken off after the roadblock. I needed to talk to you then, and I need to talk to you now."

Her hands tightened until her knuckles were white. "What about?"

"You were right. We need to talk and figure out what's going on here."

"Figure out what?" she asked in a soft voice.

He shrugged. "Everything." He couldn't keep the distance between them, and he closed the space with two long strides. She was inches from him, her fresh sweetness filling his senses. "I need to explain things."

Her tongue darted out to touch her lips before she said, "What?"

"When I was in prison, I just about gave up believing in anything. Oh, I dreamed about getting out, being free, taking off and never looking back. I could taste freedom in my dreams. But I forgot just about everything else."

"What?"

He let himself touch her chin with his index finger. "Beauty, goodness, gentleness." He exhaled. "Things I thought were lost to me forever. And that's everything you are. Everything you and Sammi embody. Everything I've lost."

She slowly lifted a hand and touched him on his chest, her palm pressed to the area of his heart. "You didn't lose it. It's there."

He looked down into her eyes. "Annie, I know what I am, what I can do, but—"

His words were cut off as Jeannie came rushing out onto the terrace with Sammi in her arms. "He's here, Annie. God, I don't know how, but Trevor's here."

One look at Annie's face and Quint knew what he was going to do. "Stay here. I'll take care of him," he said and jogged past Jeannie into the house. The front door was open and Charlie was blocking the entrance physically.

"I don't give a damn what you want, Raines, you aren't coming in my house. It's my property and you're trespassing. Your money can't buy you access—"

Quint came up behind Charlie and got his first look at Trevor Raines. The man was tall and blond, dressed in tight, black leather pants, a white silk shirt and boots that Quint didn't doubt cost upward to a thousand dollars a pair. One look at the smug smile on the man's face, and Quint could feel his adrenaline pumping.

"Let me in or I'll bring the cops. Besides, I want to see my kid. I've missed her, and I've been worried."

"You son of a—"

Quint cut off Charlie's oath with a hand on his shoulder. "Charlie, let me take care of him," he said.

"No," Annie said from behind him. "This is my problem. I'll talk to Trevor."

Quint turned and saw Annie in the middle of the room holding Sammi in her arms. He'd never seen her look like that, with her jaw set and her eyes narrowed. But even so, there was something so vulnerable in her that it made him ache. Any of his "protect the underdog" impulses paled at the strength of his need to protect this woman.

"You don't have to, Annie," Quint said.

She never looked at him. Her eyes never left Trevor. "Yes, I do. I need to tell him exactly what's going on."

Trevor pressed his advantage when they were distracted and went past Charlie and Quint into the house. "Samantha," he said as he strode across the room to where Annie stood with the baby. He held out his arms. "Come to Daddy."

Sammi cringed back against Annie, her arm going around her mother's neck. "Go way, go way," she said, a whine in her voice as her tiny hand waved at him.

"Sweetheart, Daddy came to see you," he said and reached out to take Sammi. "Come see me."

"Go way, go way," the baby sobbed, but Trevor managed to take her out of Annie's arms. Then Sammi started to scream and frantically fought against Trevor holding her. "It's all right, Samantha, Daddy came to see you."

"Mommy, Mommy," she sobbed.

"Trevor, give her back to me," Annie said tightly.

Jeannie stepped closer. "Trevor, don't do this. She's just a baby, and she doesn't even really know you. She's terrified."

He looked at Sammi's contorted face, then at Jeannie. "That's just it, she needs to learn who her father is."

Annie's face was ashen, and the pain in her eyes was too much for Quint to endure. Quint stepped in and reached for Sammi. He had her in his arms before Trevor knew what was happening, then turned and handed the crying child to Annie. The baby scrambled back to her mother and held on to her for dear life.

When Trevor grabbed Quint by the arm, Quint spun around and he knew he could kill the man.

Trevor backed up, both hands up in front of him, getting out of reach, but he wasn't backing down. "Who in the hell do you think you are? That's my kid."

"And she's upset," Quint said, his hands so tightly clenched that they ached. "Everyone is. So, why don't you go, and you can talk to Annie later when things are calmer?"

"I'm not leaving," Trevor said, then looked at Annie. "You're in real trouble . . . unless we can work things out."

She smoothed Sammi's fine blonde hair with a hand that was shaking. "You know I didn't assault you, Trevor."

"You left me for dead."

"You stumbled and passed out. You were drunk."

"Not that drunk."

Annie glanced at Quint, her eyes wide in her pale face, and he had to force himself not to grab Trevor and throw him out bodily. Then Annie looked back at Trevor. "So, you called the cops and—"

"That's not important. What's important is I'm here and we need to work things out." He almost sounded sincere. "Come back with me, and maybe we can make this work."

"How can we work out anything when you sent someone to Jeannie's to take Sammi?"

"I just wanted to have her with me, to protect her." He had an answer for everything. "I wanted her with my folks." He moved even closer and his voice dropped a bit. "And they want us all together."

Annie's paleness was increasing at an alarming rate. And even Sammi was feeling it. The crying started again, and nothing Annie did could soothe her daughter. Jeannie went to Annie. "Let's take her back in the kitchen to calm her down. *Then* you can talk with Trevor."

Annie looked from Trevor to Quint. Quint wanted to hold her close and tell her everything would be all right. But instead, he nodded to her to leave.

"I'll... I'll be right back," she said and left with Sammi and Jeannie.

"Don't you try anything," Trevor called after her. "I've got people watching the house."

Quint wanted to hit the man, but he made himself stay still. Charlie's the one who spoke up. "Who've you got out there?"

"Mason Downs, my attorney. I didn't want to bring a squad of cops, but I wasn't about to come here without backup or an impartial third party."

"Your attorney's impartial?" Charlie said.

"As much as anyone is around here."

Charlie stared at Trevor, then unexpectedly excused himself. "I've got something I need to take care of. I'll be right back."

Charlie left the room in the direction of the bedrooms, and Quint looked at Trevor. All he wanted to do was hit hard, hit quick and hit dirty.

"Just you and me. This is actually perfect," Trevor said.

"What?"

"We need to talk."

"You know, there *is* something I'd like to say to you."

Trevor cocked his head to one side. "What's that?"

"Back off, drop the charges and leave Annie and the baby alone."

"Or?" Trevor asked as a smirking smile tugged at his lips.

"Or I'll make you wish you were never born. It won't be pushing over a drunk, either." His hands clenched at his sides. "And trust me, all the Raines money isn't going to help you if I ever start on you."

"Oh, you're wrong. Money does help."

"You can buy the cops—"

"Oh, that wasn't for money, that was for my family. The Raineses are held in high esteem in and around our county. I don't know if Annie mentioned it, but my father's being recruited to run for governor by one of the major political parties. Most people know my family's good for the county and the state."

"Do I applaud now, or later?"

"Why don't you save that until I tell you some information I was able to get?"

Quint stared at him. "What information?"

"When the cops found out Annie was in the Corvette, they ran a check on the plates. Guess what? They found out you're a convicted felon who was thrown into prison for beating the hell out of a talk show host in Boston. A felon released on parole just days ago. A felon who evaded arrest, lied to the cops...you name it. I'd say you're a man who's up the creek without a paddle. Hell, you don't even have a canoe."

Quint kept his gaze steady even though his stomach was clenching. "You did your homework. But it doesn't mean a hell of a lot."

"You don't get it, do you?"

"Then spit it out."

"I can understand you picking up Annie on the road. You've been in prison. She's not hard on the eyes. And if she wants to pay her fare with you by sleeping with you, to tell you the truth, I don't give a damn."

"You son of a bitch," Quint rasped as he took a step toward Trevor.

He could see Trevor brace himself, but the man kept his voice level. "I've seen the way you look at her. Don't tell me you aren't getting what you want." He held up both hands, palms out. "But, listen to me. I'm taking both Anne Marie and the kid back with me, and you're left with two choices."

Even this man could see what was happening, and that made Quint feel sick. He kept silent, waiting for Trevor to finish.

"If you leave right now and don't look back, I'll take the heat off you. I'll tell the cops to forget you were ever involved in this mess. And they will."

"I don't give a damn what you tell the cops."

"Your second choice," he said as if Quint hadn't interrupted, "is to stay with Annie. Actually, that's probably my preference. Because if you do, I'll go to court and get full custody of my daughter once her mother's behind bars. I'll press charges and throw in the fact that she's been consorting with a known felon. I'll make sure you get thrown back in prison, and I'll get custody of Samantha. Anne Marie gets nothing except to experience what you just left."

If the man had hit Quint in the stomach with his fist, he couldn't have devastated him more. He didn't care about himself anymore. But he wouldn't let this man destroy Annie by locking her up or by taking her child. The pain on her face when Trevor had pulled Sammi out of her arms still haunted him. "Damn you, Annie's a good mother. She doesn't deserve this."

"Who cares? One way or another, I'll make sure she never sees the kid again."

Coldness began to creep into Quint's being and the dark loneliness of the prison was coming back with insidious determination. "What happens to Annie and Sammi if I get out of your way?"

"I'll take Anne Marie back, get married and make everyone happy."

"And what if Annie won't marry you?"

"I think once she sees what I can do for her, she'll agree to come back. She came once. She'll do anything for the kid, and I can do everything for the kid. Plus I'll keep Anne Marie out of jail. Then my folks will have their family all together. They can be very generous when they're happy."

"I bet you make sure Mommy and Daddy are damn happy with you," Quint muttered.

"They like the idea of me being a married man and giving them their only grandchild." He eyed Quint. "So, what's your choice?"

Quint knew he could take Annie and Sammi and run, but it would never stop. And sooner or later, everything would catch up with them and Annie would lose Sammi. He loved her too much to do that to her. And he loved her too much to let Trevor tear Sammi away from her. Not when he had the power to stop it from happening.

"All right, you've got all the cards." He took a half step closer to Trevor. "But, know this. If you ever try to take that child away from Annie, I'll come back and kill you."

Trevor's smile faltered just a bit. "You're crazy."

"No, I'm a man who doesn't have a damn thing left to lose."

"Get the hell out of here now," Trevor blustered, "or all bets are off."

Quint relished the touch of fear in the man's eyes, but nothing could make up for what was ahead. How could he just walk away? He'd thought he could before, but now he wasn't sure at all.

Then Charlie came back into the room and paused by the door. He eyed Trevor. "What's going on?"

"Mr. Gallagher's just leaving."

Charlie looked at Quint. "Is that true?"

Quint took a rough breath. "I have to, but would you do me a favor?"

"Anything," Charlie said.

Quint crossed to where the man stood, then reached in his pocket and took out some folded bills that he held out to him. "Give this to Annie for me. Tell her it's just something for her to have for a rainy day."

Charlie took the money and pushed it in his pant pocket. "Are you sure you can't stay?"

"I can't. One more thing?"

"Sure."

"Would you tell Annie—"

"Tell me what?" Annie asked.

He turned and she was at the kitchen door, tension in her expression and a vulnerability in her stance that tore at him.

"The man's leaving," Trevor said before Quint could say a thing.

Annie came slowly into the room, but stopped with the couch between herself and the men. She never looked at Trevor or Charlie. "You're going?" she asked Quint.

Quint wished that the light in here wasn't so good that her image was burning into his mind and soul. God, he knew this would be hard, but he never thought it would feel as if it were going to be fatal.

"It's time," he said simply.

"But you said we needed to sort things out."

"There's really nothing to sort out between us," he said, the lie all but choking him. "You've got your hands full here. And I've got a life I've put on hold for too long."

The paleness was there again making her wildly curling hair all the more brilliant. Her eyes darted to Trevor. "What did you say to him while I was gone?"

Quint never looked away from Annie when Trevor spoke. "Nothing. I was waiting for you to come out so we can talk."

She moved abruptly, coming around the couch and Quint almost stopped breathing when she got close to him. "Why are you leaving now?"

He narrowed his eyes, trying to take the edge off the impact of her closeness. "I told you, I'm short on time. I need to get out of here and deal with my own problems. I hope things work out for you and Sammi."

She didn't cry or beg or even yell at him in anger. Instead, he could see her literally tightening from the inside out and her arms went around herself. She'd told him she'd dealt with life on her own for years, and he realized that part of that strength came from her willing herself to deal with whatever came. And he wanted nothing more than to hold her to him and make that go away.

"Thank you for all you did," she said in a flat voice.

"Sure," he said. Then he foolishly allowed himself one last luxury. He reached out and touched her chin with the tips of his fingers. The touch was slight and barely qualified as contact, but it sent a shock wave through Quint. He caught his breath when she jerked back to break the touch almost immediately.

"Have a good life," he whispered as his hand slowly fell to his side. "You deserve it."

He turned away and crossed the room to go back to the bedroom where he'd spent the night. Once in the room, he grabbed his things and pushed them in his duffel bag. Only taking time to steady himself with a deep breath, he went back out and down the hall to the living room.

Sammi and Jeannie were there now, the child and woman sitting on the rug in front of the couch, and Annie stood over them. Trevor was sitting in one of the leather chairs, and Charlie was on the couch. Quint strode across the room. "Thanks for everything," he said to no one in particular and kept walking for the door.

"Kint!" Sammi called out.

He closed his eyes, then turned, making very sure he didn't look at Annie. The little girl was on her feet holding a rag doll in her arms and looking at him with eyes that echoed her mother's deep green. "Sammi, you be a good girl for your Mommy, okay?"

"Sammi, good girl," she echoed seriously.

"Yes, you are," he said. "I have to go. Bye-bye, Sammi."

"Quint?"

He had to look at Annie. "What?"

Silently she crossed the room to where he stood, then held something out to him. "Take this."

He looked down at the money he'd given to Charlie. "I want you to have it."

When he didn't reach for it, she dropped it at his feet. "I told you, I don't want your money," she said.

Quint looked down at Annie, and he knew he didn't belong here. He never had. Ignoring the money on the floor, he turned and left.

Another car was parked by the Corvette and a balding man was standing beside it leaning against the front fender. Trevor's attorney. Quint walked right to the Corvette, but when he touched the door handle of his car, he looked at the attorney. The man looked incredibly uncomfortable in his three-piece suit, standing on muddy ground, using his hand to shield his eyes from the sun.

"Downs?" Quint asked.

The man nodded.

"I'm Quint Gallagher."

"I know."

"Tell your client that I meant what I said to him in there."

"Just what did you say?"

"That he'd better behave himself or Mommy and Daddy aren't the only people who'll tear into him."

The man frowned, but Quint cut off any retort by getting in the car. With the top up since the storm, the interior was musty with dampness and suffocating for him so he couldn't get air in his chest. He started the engine, then quickly put the top down and finally took a deep breath.

He backed up, then turned around and started down the driveway. For a second, over the sounds of the engine and the moving air, he thought he heard his name called, and he looked in the side mirror.

The attorney was still by the car looking up at the house. Quint twisted to look over his shoulder, and he saw Annie on the porch holding one of the uprights watching him leave. And the sight of her reminded him of that first time he'd driven away from her, leaving her standing on the side of the road.

But this time she wasn't alone. She had her child. It was he who was totally alone. He looked away and pressed the gas pedal, squealing the tires on the pavement. When he got to the end of the drive, he turned onto the road.

He drove away, as alone as the day he left the prison in Boston. But now he truly felt the loneliness. It ate at him, producing a pain that he'd never experienced before.

Lifting his face to the rushing air, he screamed a curse to the skies, a curse born of pain and anger. And the sound was snatched away by the wind as it tore out of his throat, gone the next instant as if it had never been uttered.

It was about as real as the dreams he'd started to let himself dream. One minute they were there, the next they were gone as if they had never been. He ran a hand roughly over his face and knew that he'd never dream again.

Chapter Fifteen

Annie watched Quint drive away and the ache in her middle threatened to explode and consume her. She called out to him, needing to face him alone and rage at him over the money. Then she saw the car slow, Quint glance over his shoulder at her and, for a split second, she thought he was going to turn around and come back.

But that never happened. Instead, the car surged forward, its engine roaring, then he was gone and the emptiness around her pressed against her. Slowly she turned and went back into the house, her eyes painfully dry as she stopped in the doorway. Trevor was still there like a bad dream, and Jeannie was playing with Sammi on the rug. Her friend looked up.

"Is he gone?"

"Yes." She swallowed hard. "Trevor and I need to talk," she said. "Could you take Sammi out for a walk?"

Charlie stood. "I contacted my attorney, and if you—"

"I need to do this on my own." The way she had everything else in her life, except for a few days when a man named Quint had been there for her.

As Jeannie, Charlie and Sammi left through the terrace doors, Annie looked at Trevor. Suddenly she didn't care why he did what he did, or what he thought or even what he thought of her. All she cared about was Sammi. She had nothing to lose anymore except her daughter.

She crossed to the couch and looked down at Trevor. She knew she'd do anything it took to keep Sammi and to keep her safe. But she couldn't fight the Raineses' wealth, so she had to do this without a war.

"Annie, I wish we could turn back the clock—"

"Forget the games, Trevor. I know you don't love me or Sammi, and the only reason you wanted to marry me was to appease your mother and father. So why don't you tell me exactly what you want and what I get in return?"

Trevor sank back and stretched his arms out on the back of the couch at either side of himself. His eyes narrowed. "God, you've changed."

She felt like a completely different woman than the one who'd believed his lies so easily just days ago. "You haven't."

He shrugged. "Simply put, I want you and the kid to come back to the ranch with me. We tell my parents we've got everything settled. We get married."

The thought of Trevor ever touching her again made her physically ill and she had to fight sickness burning the back of her throat. "Marriage?"

"Don't look so uneasy. We'll put on a show for the folks. That's it."

"And if I don't agree to go back?"

He sat forward and rested his elbows on his knees, then tented his fingers and pressed them to his lips.

"Bluntly put, I get the kid, and you get zip except a jail cell."

She'd known all along that that was what he wanted, but it made her blood run cold to hear it laid out this way. And she didn't have any options. Quint had robbed her of options when he drove away without her. And for a second she hated Quint with a passion that almost equaled her love for him.

"You've got your attorney outside?"

"Yes."

"Then get him. I want this done legally so you can't get me back there and decide to do whatever you want to do."

He frowned up at her. "You're getting pretty cold, Anne Marie."

"You taught me well."

Two weeks later

ANNIE STOOD VERY STILL as Marla Clark, the seamstress, put the final touches on the simple white calf-length dress. This wedding dress was plain, with cap sleeves, a softly gathered skirt and a scooped neckline. Plain, and nothing like the original gown that was packed away somewhere in the main house.

"And I was telling my friend, Alice, that she wouldn't believe what's been happening out here. So romantic," she babbled. "Just wonderful. Him going after you and bringing you back and you two still getting married."

Annie felt her nerves stretch even further and it was all she could do not to tell the woman to shut up. "Are you almost done?" she asked.

"Just a minute longer," the woman said around a pin she held in her mouth.

Annie closed her eyes, then looked out the side window of the guest house. The day was bright and sunny, without a cloud in the sky, and across the rolling grass area she could see Sammi with Trevor, Senior. The older man, a weathered version of Trevor, had Sammi on his horse with him, riding her all over the grounds. Both child and adult were laughing.

A sight like that eased Annie a bit. Sammi was happy, and Trevor's parents doted on her. Maybe this could work. Maybe she could make a life here where Sammi had Mamaw and Poppa, and horses and toys and space to run and play.

Annie looked away from the view and realized that Marla was still talking. "... and I said to Alice, the Raines family is under this lucky sign. You know, the way some people are, where no matter what, everything works out for them?"

A lucky sign? Annie almost laughed at that.

"And Alice says that she'd heard that you and Trevor are going to Europe for your honeymoon, and that you're going to be gone for months traveling."

She took a breath and looked up at Annie, meeting her eyes in the mirror, waiting for some confirmation so she could go and tell it to Alice. Annie wondered what the woman would tell her friend if she was absolutely truthful.

What if she told her that there wouldn't be a honeymoon, that right after the wedding she and Trevor would move into the west wing of the house, into separate rooms joined by a luxurious bathroom? That for the month they were supposed to be on their honeymoon, Trevor had agreed to let her take Sammi back to Jeannie and Charlie to visit and that he'd meet her there in a month and they'd come back here together?

"We'll be gone a month," Annie said.

The woman looked expectantly at Annie. "A month? Then you'll be going pretty far?"

Light-years away from this place, she thought, and almost couldn't wait for the day after tomorrow when she could go back to sanity for a brief period of time. Jeannie and Charlie were already at Los Olivos, and part of Annie wondered what it would be like going back to the last place she'd seen Quint.

Just the thought of the man brought every good intention tumbling down. He'd been gone two weeks, but it could have been an eternity. And it still hurt. The old saying about time healing all wounds was proving untrue. If anything, it hurt more now than that last sight of him, turning, seeing her, then leaving.

She closed her eyes so tightly bright colors exploded behind her lids. "Your friend thinks we're going to Europe?"

"Yes, ma'am."

"Tell her she's wrong."

"The Bahamas?"

Annie opened her eyes and looked at the woman. "It's a secret. You know, we can't let people know where we'll be."

"Oh, yes," the woman said with a knowing smile. "And I'd be the same way, what with a handsome husband like yours. I'd be wanting him all to myself."

"A very good idea."

Annie saw the flash of movement in the mirror at the same time Trevor spoke. She saw his reflection in the mirror and wondered if Marla still thought he was handsome. It was barely past noon and Trevor was drunk...again. Since they'd come back, he'd been drinking nonstop, but it worked for her. He'd disappear and leave her and Sammi alone. She really didn't care if he drank himself to death.

Right now his face was flushed, his chambray shirt open and untucked, and his chinos looked mussed, as if he'd slept in them. And he probably had. "So, do you want me all to yourself?" he asked, his voice vaguely slurred as he gripped the doorframe with one hand.

Marla stood and Annie watched her smile brightly at Trevor. "Oh, sir, I'm sorry. I was just talking and you know—"

His eyes in the reflection were on Annie, and he didn't even look at the seamstress as he spoke to her. "Goodbye, Marla."

"Sir, I'm almost finished, and—"

He stood straight. "Goodbye," he bit out.

Annie cringed at his tone, and at the way Marla colored as she hurriedly picked up the supplies by her. "Yes, sir," she murmured.

Annie hated Trevor's power and the way he had to use it, even over someone like Marla.

"The dress?" Marla said to Annie.

"I'll take it off and bring it up to the house in a few minutes. Mrs. Raines wants to talk to you about Sammi's dress."

"Yes, ma'am," Marla murmured picking up her carrying tray. "I'll be waiting." She headed for the door, ducking past Trevor like a frightened mouse.

When the woman was gone and Annie could see her heading across the grass to the main house, she turned and looked at Trevor without using the reflection in the mirror as a buffer. "What do you want?"

He let go of the door and came farther into the room, his steps a bit unsteady. "What would you do if I said I wanted you?"

Bile rose bitterly at the back of her throat. "I'd say you were drunk."

"Oh, I've had a few drinks...here and there...now and then."

"Then go and sleep it off."

He stopped in front of her and the smell of whiskey hung in the air. "Are you propositioning me?"

Part of her had known this would happen sooner or later, but she'd hoped it would be much later. "No, I'm not."

"Well, damn, why not? We had some pretty great sex at first, why not let's try it again?"

They had little to nothing at first, and Annie couldn't really remember much about it. Not when memories of Quint just overlapped every other memory. For a moment, the image of Quint was so strong in her mind that she almost couldn't breathe. His touch on her, his closeness, heat everywhere, taking her, connecting in a way she'd never connected with another man in her life.

"We've got an agreement," she said, her voice vaguely husky.

He eyed her. "Yeah, but you're kind of flushed. You remember."

His voice made her sick. "I remember we've got an agreement, and part of that agreement is that this is going to be a marriage in name only."

"Screw the agreement," he muttered thickly and reached out for her.

Annie jerked back. "Stop it."

He drew his hand back and it curled into a fist. "What are you going to do, be celibate for the rest of your life?"

Without Quint, there wasn't any man she wanted. But her loving him hadn't made him love her. "That's none of your business, as long as I keep up my end of the bargain."

"Don't think you're going to find someone like that jerk you were with."

"I told you—"

Trevor rocked forward on the balls of his feet and the odor of whiskey got stronger. "Don't even think about it. I'll get rid of any jerk you find. I got rid of one, and I'll get rid of any others that come along."

She stared at Trevor. "You got rid of whom?"

"That jailbird."

"What?"

Trevor looked uncertain for a second, then he seemed to stand taller. He nodded as if he'd found a cure for cancer. "You heard me. He threatened me and everything, but he's the one who turned tail and ran. Some big man," he sneered. "He crumbled."

Annie felt as if she couldn't breathe. "What did you do to Quint?"

He shrugged. "Just told him the way it was."

She wanted to grab Trevor and shake him. "Trevor, what did you do?"

"I got rid of him," he muttered, the words slurring more and more. "I gave him a choice, and he made the right decision." He eyed her up and down. "He obviously was looking out for himself. Can't blame him. We all do. But he walked on you, didn't he?"

And he'd torn her heart out in the process. "He left."

"Yeah, he sure did. He ran."

She couldn't breathe now. Her heart was hammering against her ribs. If she could make some sense out of Quint leaving, maybe she could let him go. "Tell me why you think he left."

He shrugged. "I know why. I told him if he walked out of there, I'd fix it with the cops that they wouldn't go after him."

So, Quint had been saving his own tail, and in some way that made horrible sense. But she knew in some part of her that there had to be more. "That was all?"

"I told him to clear out and I'd get you to come back with me. That's all I wanted. He understood completely when I told him I'd take the kid and put you in jail right alongside of him if he didn't get scarce."

She had her answer. "You told him you'd take Sammi?"

"I figured he didn't want to go back inside, and the idea of you going along with him didn't sit well. Sure, I told him I'd take the kid and give you to him." He actually laughed. "He obviously didn't want you."

Annie knew a hatred of this man so pure and focused that it seemed almost spiritual. Trevor had hit all the right buttons, with both Quint and herself. And it hurt like hell that Quint walked away *for* her, not *from* her. It hurt, yet at the same time, it was exquisitely wonderful.

"You didn't want me."

"Oh, I wouldn't say that. I wouldn't be opposed to making this marriage workable, if you know what I mean?"

She stared at him, his image beginning to blur. "All you ever wanted was the money, wasn't it? All you wanted was Sammi to make your parents happy and make sure you kept your inheritance."

"Come on, Annie, get real. If it works, it works."

"And you don't even really want Sammi, do you, just what she can do for you?"

"I'm sure this father thing's going to kick in ... sometime, but for now, she's my insurance policy."

Trevor destroyed the only thing she'd ever found in this world that might have been right and good and loving. And the anger crystalized into the need to strike out. She swung at his face, wanting to give him pain he'd remember for a long time, but he caught her hand with amazing speed.

He jerked her toward him and his face was infused with bright color inches from hers. "Oh, no you don't. Don't you ever try that again or I'll have you arrested," he ground out. Then he had her by her shoulders. "I think we're going to have to renegotiate this whole contract thing. And now's as good a time to start as any."

She tried to fight against him when he tried to kiss her, but his hold on her tightened into agony. "Trevor, stop. Please ... no ..."

"Oh, yes," he muttered and he pulled her against him with a jerk. "Oh, yes," he breathed, his breath moist and hot on her neck, then his mouth was on her skin and she thought she'd throw up.

"Stop that, Trevor, right now!"

He froze at the sound of his mother's voice, then pushed Annie back from him so quickly that she stumbled and barely kept herself from falling by grabbing the footboard of the bed.

Annie got her balance, then rubbed at her left shoulder as she looked past Trevor. Angelica Raines was at the open door, the tiny woman immaculately dressed in a simple beige sheath with the flash of diamonds at her throat and ears. Her silvery hair was cut short in a simple bob, and the look on her face was different than any Annie had ever seen.

The woman was always in control, always elegant and contained. But right now high color touched her cheeks and her mouth was rimmed by whiteness.

"Mother, this isn't what you think. I mean, Anne Marie and I are going to be married tomorrow and it isn't as if we haven't been together before." He laughed, a jarring sound. "That's why you've got little Samantha."

Mrs. Raines stared at Trevor and her color deepened. "Trevor, go up to the house, take a cold shower and go to bed."

He hesitated.

"Now, Trevor," she said. "Do it."

He never looked at Annie again before he walked unsteadily to the door, then went out past his mother and left. Mrs. Raines closed her eyes for a moment, then opened them, the look of distaste in her expression enough to tell Annie that she was displeased to say the least.

Mrs. Raines didn't speak as she quietly closed the door then turned to Annie. Her pale blue eyes were guarded, but the woman was in control again.

"I am truly sorry for what my son has done," she said in a well-modulated voice that held none of the flat Oklahoma twang. "I am very sorry."

Annie rubbed at her shoulder. "He's been drinking."

"The way he was before you ran away?"

"Yes."

Mrs. Raines came farther into the room, bringing the scent of very expensive perfume with her. Silently she crossed to the window and looked out. Annie could see past her to Trevor making his way across the grass to the main house. In the distance, the senior Raines was still riding Sammi on his palomino gelding.

Annie waited quietly, never able to shake the feeling that when she and Mrs. Raines met, the older lady was granting her an audience. The only time she thought the woman looked approachable was when she was with Sammi. She saw Mrs. Raines take a deep breath, then turn. "The child seems very happy," she said.

"Yes, she loves the horses and riding."

Mrs. Raines hesitated, then got right to the point. "I was at the door. I heard what Trevor said to you."

Annie went around and sat down on the side of the bed, then looked across the room at the tiny woman. "Did you hear everything?"

"I heard enough. Did he force you to come back here?"

She bit her lip. "Mrs. Raines, I came back because—"

"My dear, please, don't try to sugarcoat what my son did. Just tell me the truth. Why did you come back here?"

"Mrs. Raines, the only important thing in my life is Sammi. She's everything to me."

"I know that. I have eyes. I see you with her, how much she loves you and how much you love her. And we love her, my dear, believe me. She's the brightest ray of sunshine in our world. But I need to understand what's going on. Tell me why you left and why you came back."

Annie took an unsteady breath, then told the woman the truth. "Trevor said that if I didn't come back and go through with the marriage that he'd take Sammi away from me and have me locked up for that...accident in the stables."

"Oh, my God." Mrs. Raines came across the room to where Annie sat on the bed. Unexpectedly she sank down by her, and for the first time since they'd met, she touched Annie. Her cool hand covered Annie's in her lap. "Just tell me everything," she said softly.

Annie hesitated.

"My dear, we aren't going to take Samantha, believe me. No matter what happens with Trevor. Now, talk to me."

Annie took what felt like the first free breath she'd taken in a long time. Then she told Mrs. Raines everything except about Quint. When she finished, the older lady drew back and when Annie looked at her, Trevor's mother looked ashen.

"Trevor did all that?"

"Yes."

"I knew he was selfish and immature, but to hurt you like that and to use that sweet child..." She shook her head. "I never, never dreamed he'd do anything like that."

"I couldn't let him take Sammi."

"No, no of course not." Mrs. Raines stood again and crossed to the window. She stood with her back to

Annie for a very long time, then asked, "And the man you were with?"

"He's gone."

"Was he important to you?"

"Yes," she said simply.

"Did you love him, my dear?"

Tears burned her eyes and Annie had a hard time forming the single word a second time. "Yes."

"Did he love you?"

"I thought...I don't really know. He left so abruptly."

"He was in jail?"

She didn't see any reason to lie, so she told Mrs. Raines about Quint. When she finished, the older woman finally turned to Annie. "And Samantha, does he care about her?"

She thought of his last look at Sammi, the expression on his face. "Yes, I think he does."

Mrs. Raines came back to the bed but didn't sit this time. She stood over Annie and when Annie looked up, the woman smiled at her, a smile touched with sadness. "I was hoping that we could be a family, you and Trevor and my husband and me, and mostly Samantha. We truly love her, you must know that."

She didn't doubt that. "I know."

"She's very important to us, dear, but if I had known what Trevor..." She closed her eyes for a moment, and Annie thought the woman looked old. Beyond the elegance and control, the woman was in pain, a pain Annie finally knew came from Trevor.

For the first time since Quint had walked out, Annie felt as if the world wasn't on its ear. It was unsteady, but not about to crash. "He said he'd take

Sammi away, that I'd be locked up and never see her again."

"Let's get something very clear. I apologize for what my son has done to you, and I promise you that he was not speaking for this family. You're Samantha's mother. That's the way it should be and will always be. All I ask is that you allow my husband and me to be grandparents to her."

It couldn't be that simple. "What about Trevor?"

Her mouth thinned. "We will take care of Trevor."

"But I signed an agreement with him—"

Mrs. Raines touched Annie on the cheek. "Oh, my dear, forget about anything you agreed to with Trevor. Trust me, nothing he said or did is important now." Her hand was unsteady. "Just make the life you want for you and the child. And let us be a part of it."

The life she wanted? "I don't know..." Her words faltered, then she managed, "If that new life could be with Quint, would it matter to you?"

"As long as he's good to Samantha, that's all that matters. Now, figure out what that life is going to be. This life is too short to be proud or to let anything get in your way."

Annie could see the old steel coming back in the woman, both in her tone and the way she held herself. "You're right. Life is short."

"You'll be leaving, won't you?"

"Yes, I need to."

"I know. Just promise me that you'll always let us be part of the child's life."

"I promise you that."

"I'll go and find my husband and Samantha, then have her things packed. Do you need a ride to the airport?"

"Yes, if it wouldn't be too much trouble."

"The car will be ready. May I ask where you're going?"

"Santa Barbara, California."

GETTING THROUGH the days was hard for Quint but not as hard as the nights. When sleep started to come, images of Annie came with it and the memories of the short time he had with her tore at any peace he managed to gather around him.

He'd worked at his brother's body shop since arriving in town, putting in long hours and putting off that time when he had to leave and go back to the small apartment he'd found near the harbor. Sometimes when he couldn't face the emptiness, he got in his car and drove.

He'd found Annie's picture in the car after he left her, and he kept it in the console compartment. He never even looked at it again, but every time he got in the car, he knew it was there.

It was almost seven-thirty on a Friday evening when he finally walked out the door of the body shop and locked up after him. He was the last one to leave, the way he usually was, and as he turned the key in the lock, he knew that he wasn't going back to the apartment tonight. A drive up the coast would numb him a bit before he faced the emptiness.

He turned, the tangy scent of the nearby ocean hanging in the cooling air. He started across to where he'd parked the Corvette under an old pepper tree, the shadows almost hiding the black car. As Quint headed for it, his stride slowed when he saw a sight he knew couldn't be real. Had his dreams suddenly come to life? Sitting contentedly as you please in the car was Annie.

Chapter Sixteen

Quint stopped five feet from the car, closed his eyes, then took a deep breath and opened them again. Annie was still there, watching him, waiting for him. It was as if he were thrown back in time to that moment when he ran out of the truck stop after the fight. Annie had been waiting in the car for him, expecting him to take her off into the night.

He narrowed his eyes, barely able to bear the sight his mind was conjuring up for him. Annie, her hair loose and curling wild, her expression lost in the deep shadows.

"Annie?" he breathed, wondering if the sound of him speaking out loud would make her dissolve into thin air.

"Hi, Quint," she said, and her voice sounded real enough.

As the truth of her presence sank in, the love that he'd thought he was beginning to deal with was there with a force that left him breathless. "You . . . you're here."

"Yes, and I'm waiting for a ride," she said softly.

His promise to Trevor was something he took seriously. And right after he got here, he had a private investigator in Oklahoma find out about Annie. She was set to marry Trevor in a quiet, private ceremony. The wedding was supposed to be today. "I thought you . . . were with Trevor, that you were getting married."

"I was supposed to marry Trevor today."

"You didn't take off again, did you?"

"Actually, I did."

"God, Annie, what in the—"

"I couldn't marry him," she said. "I left, but this time I flew. The odds were I couldn't find a poor innocent person driving a terrific black car who could be forced to give me a ride and help me lay low."

She almost sounded as if this were funny to her. "Annie, you can't—"

"Why, because Trevor told you if I didn't go with him and marry him that he'd take Sammi from me and have me locked up?"

He felt rooted to the spot. "What?"

"He told you if you didn't leave me, that he'd take Sammi, didn't he?"

"That doesn't matter right now."

"You lied to me. You told me that you didn't want to be involved, that you were on your own, every man for himself and all that stuff. And all the time, you left because you were afraid that Trevor would take Sammi if you didn't walk out."

"Annie, don't do this."

She climbed over the closed passenger door of the car and came around to where he stood. This close to him, she seemed more delicate than he remembered, but that same scent came with her, fresh, sweetness that touched the evening air. It seemed as if he'd been just biding his time until this moment, but now it was here, he didn't know what to do.

Every part of him wanted to reach out and hold her to him, to remember the feeling of having her in his arms. But this time, if he touched her, he wasn't going to be noble and let her go. Never again. So he pushed his hands behind his back and clenched them into fists.

"I have to do this, Quint. If I don't, I'll probably go crazy."

He was close enough to crazy that he probably wouldn't notice it in her anyway. "You need to go back, Annie. You can't do this."

"What I need are answers. I need to know if you care about Sammi."

The answer came easily. "Of course I care about her."

"Good." She released a soft breath. "Now, I need to know one more thing, and you have to tell me the truth."

"What?" he asked, barely able to take air into his lungs.

"Do you love me?"

He turned from her and uttered a low curse that shattered the night. "Get the hell out of here," he muttered. "You can't take the chance of losing Sammi. I won't let you, not after everything that's happened."

Every defense he had built in him to keep his distance was shattered when he felt her touch him on the back. Even through the cotton of his shirt, the contact was electric, and he jerked forward, then turned on her. "Don't do that again. I told you I'm looking out for myself. And you really are crazy jeopardizing everything by being here."

She came even closer, but even though she didn't touch him again, she was filling his world as surely as he needed air and water to live. "Just answer me, please, do you love me?"

"What do you want from me?" he demanded.

"If you don't love me, say so right now. If you do, I need to know."

He looked up at the heavens, at a dark sky that held no answers for him. Then he looked back at Annie. He wished he could lie, that he could say the words that would send her back to Trevor once again, but he couldn't. He couldn't say he didn't love her when just being this close to her seemed to fill in all the empty blackness in his soul. "All right. The truth."

"Please," she begged softly.

"I love you, Annie. I have since we met, and I've got a sneaking suspicion I will until I die."

She was motionless for a single heartbeat, then she was in his arms. He thought he'd given up on dreams, but this was one dream he wasn't going to question. He held her to him, desperate for the feeling of her body against his, the feeling of her filling his arms, the way she smelled and the softness of her voice against his chest.

"Thank you, thank you, thank you," she whispered and he could feel her shaking.

He laced his fingers in her tangled hair and gently eased her head back until she had to look up at him. The pleasure in her expression couldn't be hidden by the night, and for that moment he let himself feel things that he'd told himself he'd never allow himself to feel again.

"Oh, Annie, of course I love you. How couldn't I? But you can't give up Sammi. And Trevor's going to take her if he even suspects that you're here."

"Kint!"

The sound of the child's voice came from the car, and Quint looked past Annie. Sammi stood on the driver's seat, clutching the doorframe and bouncing on the leather. "You took her with you?"

"Of course I did," Annie said. "I wasn't about to ever leave her. And I told her all about you on the way here. I think she remembered on her own, but I wanted her to know how important you are to me."

"Talk about a bad case of stupidity," he muttered as he let Annie go to cross to the car.

The child stood on the driver's seat and her doll was at her feet. "Sammi," he said.

As soon as he said her name, she held out her arms. "Hold, peeze," she said. "Kint, hold peeze?"

He knew he was falling down into a place where he'd never be able to get out, but he reached out and lifted Sammi into his arms. "Kint, fie, airpain, airpain. Up in sky."

Quint turned when he sensed Annie close behind him, and he found her right there, watching him with her child and tears were staining her cheeks. He had no options at all, not one.

"All right. You're here. What's the plan?"

"To be with you, if you'll have us."

"Annie, that's a fantasy. It's a delusion."

"No, this is real. Trevor's parents know all about what he did, and they gave me their blessings. They won't take Sammi, as long as they can be in her life. Now, all that's left for me is to know if we have a life with you."

Whatever dream he was having was a dream he never wanted to wake from. He reached out for her with his free hand. "Oh, God, I've never wanted anything more than I want a life with you...with both of you."

She pressed a hand to her mouth, then quietly buried her face in his chest. Sammi patted her head. "Mommy sad? Mommy sad?"

Annie took a shuddering breath, then looked up and met Quint's gaze. "No, Sammi, Mommy's not sad. Not anymore."

Quint dipped his head and found her lips with his. Her taste, mingled with tears of joy, filled him and he knew that all the loneliness and sadness in his life had just been banished.

QUINT LOOKED UP as Annie walked into the bedroom on the second floor of the old, rambling house in the hills overlooking Santa Barbara. They'd rented it the day after she and Sammi arrived, and it already felt like home.

Quint watched her come toward the bed, her hair loose and curling around her face. She was wearing a short robe, and her feet were bare. As she stopped by him where he sat on the bed, he could feel a response to her presence that never ceased to amaze him.

For the past two weeks, he'd been living his life instead of enduring it. He'd worked and come home and played with Sammi and made love to Annie, and he knew that life couldn't possibly get any better.

She looked down at him in the soft light from the single bedside lamp. "That was Mrs. Raines on the phone. She would absolutely adore having Sammi for a week while we go on our honeymoon. They have big plans for celebrating her birthday a few weeks late. And they'll spoil her rotten."

"What about Trevor?"

She reached out and touched his cheek, the contact as potent as any had ever been. "He won't be there. He's been quietly admitted to an alcohol recovery program, and..." Her fingers traced the line of his jaw. "Maybe they can help him grow up a bit."

"There wasn't any problem when you told them we were married?"

Her finger trembled as it touched his lips. "A bit of regret, but they were fine. And having Sammi with them sort of makes up for a lot of things."

He reached up and circled her waist with his hands and pulled her down onto his lap. As she put her arm around his neck, he laughed softly. "Do you remember the last time you sat on my lap?"

She touched her lips to a sensitive spot by his ear then whispered, "Of course, but this isn't a bus station or a tiny stall that frustrated every natural instinct. We've got a huge bed."

Her laughter sounded like music to him as they tumbled together into the coolness of the linen. "Natural instincts? Amen to natural instincts," he murmured as he found her lips and kissed her with a fervor that just never diminished.

She responded with as much urgency as was in him, and somehow their clothes were gone and they were lying with each other, skin against skin, all barriers gone. Quint tasted her neck and shoulders, then found her breasts and when he felt her nipples tighten under his touch, there was no patience in him. He wanted her. He wanted her over and over and over again. And he knew that one life would never be enough to satisfy that hunger.

As if she read his mind, she touched his stomach, then trailed her hand down until she found the evidence of his desire for her. When she circled his heat, he felt sensations explode in him, and before he could shift over her, she moved. She straddled him and slowly eased herself down until he filled her.

She was still, and he looked up at her, her coppery curls falling forward, and he spanned her waist with his hands. "Oh, Annie, thank you for being here, for being my wife. When I think of Trevor and—"

"Shh," she said softly. "We're married just a few hours, and the last thing I want to talk about is Trevor."

She started to rock slowly, and the friction engulfed him in shards of sensations that blotted out everything except here and now. "Amen," he whispered and began to move.

He'd always thought dreams were a form of escape from a prison of one sort or another. Then they were over, and he was still in the prison, either the cell or a life that was empty and senseless. But not now.

Annie moved with him, her soft moans mixed with his, filling the spaces around him. And when they climaxed together, when they both cried out, then held on to each other, he knew nothing was over.

His dream was real and it was just beginning. And he was free. Really free for the first time in his life.

HARLEQUIN®

AMERICAN ❖ ROMANCE®

Once in a while, there's a story so special, a story so
unusual, that your pulse races, your blood rushes.
We call this

AMERICAN
ROMANCE
heartbeat

Borrowed Time is one such book.

Kathleen Welles receives a most unusual offer: to sell one past day in her life for a
million dollars! What she didn't realize was that she'd be transported back in time, to
the very day she'd sold—the day she lost her true love, Zachary Forest. Can she right
her wrongs and reclaim the man she loves in a mere twenty-four hours?

#574 BORROWED TIME
by
Cassie Miles

Available in March, wherever Harlequin books are sold.
Watch for more Heartbeat stories, coming your way soon!

Take 4 bestselling love stories FREE

Plus get a FREE surprise gift!

Special Limited-time Offer

Mail to Harlequin Reader Service®

3010 Walden Avenue
P.O. Box 1867
Buffalo, N.Y. 14269-1867

YES! Please send me 4 free Harlequin American Romance® novels and my free surprise gift. Then send me 4 brand-new novels every month, which I will receive months before they appear in bookstores. Bill me at the low price of $2.89 each plus 25¢ delivery and applicable sales tax, if any.* That's the complete price and a savings of over 10% off the cover prices—quite a bargain! I understand that accepting the books and gift places me under no obligation ever to buy any books. I can always return a shipment and cancel at any time. Even if I never buy another book from Harlequin, the 4 free books and the surprise gift are mine to keep forever.

154 BPA ANRL

Name	(PLEASE PRINT)	
Address	Apt. No.	
City	State	Zip

This offer is limited to one order per household and not valid to present Harlequin American Romance® subscribers. *Terms and prices are subject to change without notice. Sales tax applicable in N.Y.

UAM-295   ©1990 Harlequin Enterprises Limited

HARLEQUIN®

A M E R I C A N ◆ R O M A N C E®

IS BRINGING
YOU A BABY BOOM!

NEW ARRIVALS

We're expecting! This spring, from March through May, three very special Harlequin American Romance authors invite you to read about three equally special heroines—all of whom are on a nine-month adventure! We expect each soon-to-be mom will find the man of her dreams—and a daddy in the bargain!

So don't miss the first of these titles:

#576 BABY MAKES NINE
by Vivian Leiber
March 1995

Look for the New Arrivals logo—and please help us welcome our new arrivals!

NA-G

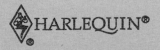

Harlequin invites you to the most
romantic wedding of the season.

Rope the cowboy of your dreams in
Marry Me, Cowboy!

A collection of 4 brand-new stories,
celebrating weddings, written by:

New York Times bestselling author

JANET DAILEY

and favorite authors

Margaret Way
Anne McAllister
Susan Fox

Be sure not to miss Marry Me, Cowboy!
coming this April

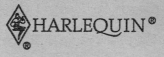 HARLEQUIN®

MMC

HARLEQUIN®

Deceit, betrayal, murder

Join Harlequin's intrepid heroines, India Leigh and Mary Hadfield, as they ferret out the truth behind the mysterious goings-on in their neighborhood. These two women are no milk-and-water misses. In fact, they thrive on

MISCHIEF & MAYHEM

Watch for their incredible adventures in this special two-book collection. Available in March, wherever Harlequin books are sold.

HARLEQUIN®

Don't miss these Harlequin favorites by some of our most distinguished authors!
And now, you can receive a discount by ordering two or more titles!

HT#25577	WILD LIKE THE WIND by Janice Kaiser	$2.99	☐
HT#25589	THE RETURN OF CAINE O'HALLORAN by JoAnn Ross	$2.99	☐
HP#11626	THE SEDUCTION STAKES by Lindsay Armstrong	$2.99	☐
HP#11647	GIVE A MAN A BAD NAME by Roberta Leigh	$2.99	☐
HR#03293	THE MAN WHO CAME FOR CHRISTMAS by Bethany Campbell	$2.89	☐
HR#03308	RELATIVE VALUES by Jessica Steele	$2.89	☐
SR#70589	CANDY KISSES by Muriel Jensen	$3.50	☐
SR#70598	WEDDING INVITATION by Marisa Carroll	$3.50 U.S. $3.99 CAN.	☐ ☐
HI#22230	CACHE POOR by Margaret St. George	$2.99	☐
HAR#16515	NO ROOM AT THE INN by Linda Randall Wisdom	$3.50	☐
HAR#16520	THE ADVENTURESS by M.J. Rodgers	$3.50	☐
HS#28795	PIECES OF SKY by Marianne Willman	$3.99	☐
HS#28824	A WARRIOR'S WAY by Margaret Moore	$3.99 U.S. $4.50 CAN.	☐ ☐

(limited quantities available on certain titles)

	AMOUNT	$
DEDUCT:	**10% DISCOUNT FOR 2+ BOOKS**	$
ADD:	**POSTAGE & HANDLING**	$
	($1.00 for one book, 50¢ for each additional)	
	APPLICABLE TAXES*	$_____
	TOTAL PAYABLE	$_____
	(check or money order—please do not send cash)	

To order, complete this form and send it, along with a check or money order for the total above, payable to Harlequin Books, to: **In the U.S.:** 3010 Walden Avenue, P.O. Box 9047, Buffalo, NY 14269-9047; **In Canada:** P.O. Box 613, Fort Erie, Ontario, L2A 5X3.

Name:_____

Address: _____ City: _____

State/Prov.:_____ Zip/Postal Code:_____

*New York residents remit applicable sales taxes.
Canadian residents remit applicable GST and provincial taxes.

HBACK-JM2